Scraps of Evidence

Other Books in the Quilts of Love Series

SCRAPS OF EVIDENCE

Quilts of Love

Barbara Cameron

Abingdon fiction™
a novel approach to faith

Other Books by the Author

A Time to Love, book one in the Quilts of Lancaster County series
A Time to Heal, book two in the Quilts of Lancaster County series
A Time for Peace, book three in the Quilts of Lancaster County series
Annie's Christmas Wish, book four in the Quilts of Lancaster County series

Her Restless Heart, book one in the Stitches in Time series
The Heart's Journey, book two in the Stitches in Time series
Heart in Hand, book three in the Stitches in Time series

And look for Amish Roads, a new Amish series starting in 2014

Scraps of Evidence

Copyright © 2014 Barbara Cameron

ISBN: 978-1-4267-5278-0

Published by Abingdon Press, P.O. Box 801, Nashville, TN 37202

www.abingdonpress.com

Published in association with the Books & Such Literary Agency.

The persons and events portrayed in this work of fiction
are the creations of the author, and any resemblance
to persons living or dead is purely coincidental.

Library of Congress Cataloging-in-Publication Data has been
requested.

Printed in the United States of America

1 2 3 4 5 6 7 8 9 10 / 19 18 17 16 15 14

For Carl

Acknowledgments

St. Augustine, Florida, the oldest city in the United States, has always inspired me with its beauty and history. When I walk around the city, I feel the stories of the men and women who founded it. A number of nations fought to own the city and impose their control and their religious principles upon it.

I love to walk around the city and admire the architecture of the old buildings, the cobblestone streets, and the immense coquina fort that defended the city. When I'm tired, I like to take one of the horse drawn carriages and listen to the guide talk about the history.

One of my favorite memories is introducing my youngest grandson—a true, modern-day kid with his love for fast electronic games—to the pleasure of a leisurely, old-fashioned ride with his mom and me.

Another memory is of walking through St. George Street in a light, silvery rain with my college friend, Carl, and enjoying Cuban food on a restaurant patio as the sun came out. I can still taste those fried plantains and feel the warmth of friendship on the rare day we found the time to get together and talk about our days at the University of Central Florida.

Those visits to St. Augustine have inspired several stories including this, my favorite. A city like this inspires stories of passion and intrigue—and faith and love. I am grateful to my editor, Ramona Richards, for believing in this story so different from my Amish novels. I hope you enjoy it!

1

Tess fought back a yawn as she walked into her aunt's hospital room. Excitement had kept her awake half the night.

"I told you that you didn't need to come," her aunt said when she saw Tess. But she smiled.

"I wanted to." She bent down and kissed her cheek. "You're my favorite aunt."

"I'm your only aunt."

"Still my favorite."

Tess pulled a chair up to the side of the bed and set the tote bag she carried on the floor. "What did the doctor say?"

"No concussion. But I have to stay another day for observation. Doctors," she muttered, her mouth turning down at the corners.

Tess studied her aunt's pale face. Sometimes when she looked at her she missed her mother so much it hurt. She didn't know what she'd do if she lost her, too.

She shook off the thought. Her aunt was just in her late fifties and in good health. There was no reason to believe she wouldn't be around for a long time.

"Big day today, huh?"

"The biggest. It's what I've been working toward since I graduated from the police academy."

Her aunt reached for her hand and squeezed it. "I'm happy for you."

"Brought you something."

"You shouldn't have. You look tired."

"Gee. Thanks." She pulled the makeup bag from the tote, and her aunt pounced on it.

"Oh, thank goodness!" Kathy cried. "They gave me a comb, but a girl needs her lipstick to feel human."

She pulled out a compact, opened it, and grimaced. "Oh, my, it's worse than I thought."

Using her forefinger, she dabbed some concealer cream on the delicate skin under one eye, then shook her head.

"Going to have a bit of a shiner there," she said with a sigh. She patted on some powder, applied some lipstick, then smiled at her appearance. "Not bad."

"You look great. No one expects you to look like a beauty queen in the hospital."

"One must keep up one's appearance," Kathy said, folding her hands primly on top of the blanket covering her.

Aunt Kathy had always reminded Tess of Grace Kelly, that icy blond actress in the old movies they'd watched together on TV years ago.

Tess was the opposite. She wore her shoulder-length blond hair in a no-nonsense twist or ponytail, hated makeup, and instead of being dainty had been five-foot-ten since high school. Oh, and there were those ten unwanted pounds that persisted in sticking around no matter what she did.

Her aunt turned the mirror on Tess. "Forgot something?"

She wanted to roll her eyes but decided not to. With a big sigh, Tess pulled a tube of lip gloss out of her pocket and swiped it across her mouth.

"My, my, don't be primping so much," her aunt said with a touch of sarcasm as Tess tucked the tube back in her pocket.

"Makeup just slides right off my face in this heat."

"I like your new look."

Tess stared down at her lightweight navy jacket and slacks worn with a crisp white shirt. She liked what it represented more. Not that she'd ever minded wearing a uniform. It was what had gotten her to this point. Now, she simply wore a different one.

"You're young," Kathy said. "I guess you don't need as much makeup as an old lady like me. And you've got those high, high cheekbones that don't need blush for emphasis. Some blue shadow would really bring out those eyes, though."

"You're not old. And I'm twenty-eight. That's not exactly young."

Tess reached down and withdrew a blue quilt from the tote bag and placed it on her aunt's lap. "I thought you might like to have it here to remind you of home."

Her aunt tried to sit up. Tess sprang out of her chair, helped raise the bed a bit and adjusted the pillow behind her aunt's head.

"Better?"

"Yes, thanks."

Tess watched as Kathy unfolded the quilt and stroked it. "It's my favorite."

"I know."

She raised a corner of it to her cheek and her eyes closed, then opened. "I'll never forget the day Gordon walked into my shop."

"He was this big, burly police officer," Tess prompted with a smile.

"So you've heard the story, eh?"

Tess laughed. "About a million times," she said.

Kathy nodded, but she smiled and didn't take offense.

"But tell it to me again." She leaned back in her chair.

"I thought he was coming to tell me I was illegally parked out front or something," her aunt said, her eyes beginning to take on a faraway look. "It was so hard to find parking because they were working on the street for the longest time. But he had this bag of clothes in his hands. Fabric scraps."

"Things that had been worn by his sister and his mother."

"Um-hmm. He thought his mother would enjoy having a quilt made of them. Mother's Day was coming up."

"So he brought in a few pieces each week and you made the quilt."

"That's right." She examined the stitching on one square and then, apparently finding it satisfactory, tucked it around her. "Something just clicked into place. We had coffee a couple of times in February, began dating. We were married by the time Mother's Day rolled around."

"So Gordon's mother got two presents."

"I don't think she saw it that way. We weren't very good friends at first. Gordon could have been a little more diplomatic about letting her know our plans to get married."

Tess felt his presence before she saw him. She wasn't sure why but it had always been so.

"What's this talk about I'm not diplomatic?" Gordon asked in his booming voice.

He strolled into the room, a tall, big-boned man. Like his wife, he was in his fifties and worked out often so his white dress shirt stretched tightly over his barrel chest.

Her aunt jumped. "Gordon! You startled me."

He just laughed, removed the toothpick dangling from his mouth and bent to kiss her head. "Oh, stop the fussing, Kathy," he drawled.

"If you hadn't done that—" she stopped, pressed her lips tightly, and plucked at the quilt.

Gordon turned to Tess. "So, hear your new partner's due in today. Big city guy, eh?"

"That's what I hear."

She watched him as he prowled around the room, peering at the bouquets her aunt had received. When he passed a mirror that hung on one wall, he peered into it critically and checked his crew cut. The short strands stood at attention on his head as if not daring to lie down on the job.

Then he began moving around the room again, as if restless. He pulled a card from an arrangement of daisies and frowned at it. "Who's this Lee?"

"A woman at church."

"You sure?"

Kathy sighed. "Yes. You met her once. Lee Weatherby."

"Hmm. Yeah. I remember. Old biddy." He tucked the card back in the bouquet and glanced at his watch. "Gotta go. I'll check in on you later."

"You can't stay for a few minutes?"

He shook his head. "Have to see the chief. We're still working out the details of my promotion. It's a big deal to be second in command, you know."

"I know. I just haven't seen you much lately."

"It'll settle down soon. I'll check in on you later." He patted her head and turned to Tess. "You working today?"

"You know I am," she said mildly.

He grinned, removed his toothpick, and tossed it in the trash. It missed, but he didn't slow down to pick it up on his way out of the room.

Tess turned to her aunt and saw she watched her husband's exit with a mixture of sadness and bewilderment.

"Aunt Kathy?" She waited until she turned to look at her. She hesitated, then plunged ahead. "Is everything okay with you and Gordon?"

She raised her eyebrows. "Of course. Why do you ask such a question?"

"I still don't know how you got hurt."

"Oh, it was so silly, really," Kathy said. "I just tripped over Prissy, that's all. She always seems to be underfoot."

Prissy was a very spoiled Persian her aunt had had for many years. Tess had never known her to hang out anywhere but the sofa and around the food bowl.

"You're sure?" Tess asked quietly.

"Of course." She looked over the side of the bed. "Now, I don't suppose you have anything else in that tote bag, do you?"

Laughing, Tess picked it up and handed it to her. Kathy grinned as she pulled out the quilt she was currently working on. Tess helped her spread it out, find her needles and thread in the sewing basket she'd brought. Then she sat back as her aunt happily began working.

"You didn't bring yours?"

Tess shook her head. "I knew I wouldn't have enough time. But maybe tomorrow. I'm off." She glanced at her watch. "I'm sorry, but I need to get going. Anything you need before I leave?"

"Not a thing. Oh, did you feed Prissy when you went by the house? Gordon forgets when I'm not home."

"Sure did." And Prissy had simply looked at her disdainfully from her place on the sofa.

Kathy held out her hands and Tess took them. "Father, walk with Tess and protect her and keep her safe. Help her to do her job to the best of her ability. Thank you. Amen."

Tess squeezed her hands and smiled, then stood and hugged her. "See you tomorrow. Call me before then if you need anything."

The heat hit her like a wet blanket the minute she left the building. Another July in St. Augustine, oldest city in the country. She was that rare thing—a native Floridian—and in all her twenty-eight years she couldn't remember a hotter one.

As much as she wanted to hurry into the air-conditioned haven of the unmarked car she'd been assigned as a detective, she forced herself not to rush. Hurrying just made it feel hotter and besides, she'd likely be out in the heat for much of the rest of the day. She started the car, turned the AC on high, and knew that she'd probably be at the station before the interior cooled off.

A sightseeing tram pulled in front of her at the light beside the police station. The driver recognized Tess, and she waved.

Tess smiled and muttered, "Hurry up," beneath her breath. Nothing was slower than the tram. Except for the horse-drawn carriages. Thankfully, none of those were in sight.

With time to spare, she pulled into the parking lot, gathered her things, and walked inside.

Maria from Records sat eating a sandwich in the break room. Tess stowed her lunch in the refrigerator.

"First day on the new job, huh? How's it feel?"

"Pretty good."

"Met the new guy yet?"

"Not yet."

Maria fanned herself with her hand. "Hot."

Tess chuckled and shook her head. "You're bad. See you later."

Two men stood just inside the roll call room, their backs turned to her.

"Ever had a female partner before?" she heard one of them ask. Tom Smithers. Figured.

"No."

Tess froze, wondering what Smithers was going to say next.

"Well, you've got your work cut out for you, buddy," Smithers said and he laughed.

The other man turned and saw Tess. Her training had taught her to capture an impression quickly and what she got was *intense*: his eyes were green and honed in on her, his posture military straight, and his stance at attention. He looked to be in his early thirties. Tall, probably six-two, and like Maria had said, he was hot: male model pretty with black hair and an easy grin.

"Aw, heck, she's right behind me, isn't she?" Smithers asked when the man grinned.

He laughed. "What do you think?"

Stepping forward, he offered his hand. "Detective Villanova. Nice to meet you. I'm Logan McMillan, your new partner."

She had a nice, firm grip and looked him straight in the eye. "Tess."

He liked the way she observed Smithers slinking off, muttering about getting some water. Maybe she was good at hiding her expression—well, actually, she better be because no cop survived without being good at keeping a nonemotional front—but she didn't waste a second on a glare at him or any kind of comment.

"Never a good idea to talk about someone," he said quietly, as she looked down at the hand he still held.

She shrugged but couldn't hold back a small smile. "And if you're going to do it, be bright enough not to stand with your back to the door."

Other officers began crowding in the door. Logan gestured for Tess to precede him in finding a seat and sat next to her. The shift supervisor went over the previous night's activity and bulletins, then introduced Logan.

He tried not to fidget as the supervisor read off his list of accomplishments. They sounded great, but in the end what did that sort of thing matter?

"So make him feel welcome to our fair city," the supervisor was saying. "Let's go out there and protect and serve, people. And stay safe."

"I think they say the same thing everywhere," he whispered to Tess.

He rose when fellow officers stopped to introduce themselves on their way out of the room. Maybe it was a stereotype, but he had expected the officers in a tourist city would look more laid-back.

The shift supervisor walked over. "Take a few hours to show Logan around, give him a feel for the city."

"Yes sir."

They walked out, and Tess stopped at the unmarked car. "Want to flip for who drives?"

"Why? I have no problem with you driving. Partner."

Her head snapped up, and she gave him a measuring look. He smiled at her and got into the car. The second look came as no surprise after the comment by Smithers. Law enforcement was still a man's world in many communities.

"We're right in the historic district here," she said as she guided the car onto King Street. "It's not a big area, and during tourist season it's crowded. You have to keep your eyes peeled or it's easy to run over a jaywalker."

She gave him the standard tour. He debated telling her he'd taken it when he visited for the interview and decided not to at this point. Seeing the city through her eyes would give him a better perspective of it—and her.

"Years ago there was quite a debate over whether a new, modern-looking bridge should replace this one. Every so often somebody would get fed up with the traffic jams on the bridge," she said as they waited at the traffic light to drive over the bridge that connected downtown St. Augustine to Anastasia Island.

"The old bridge had deteriorated," she continued. "Finally, we got a new bridge but it looks like the old one. The two Medici lions there were at the foot of the old bridge, and now they guard this one."

She turned to him and smiled. "What other city has something like this?"

The light changed and just as they were halfway across, lights flashed and a gate came down, blocking traffic. The drawbridge went up as a boat passed beneath.

"You learn to pray that we don't have an emergency and get stuck on the bridge," she said as she drummed her fingers on the steering wheel.

The drive was short since the island was small. "If you're into lighthouses, you'll have to climb this one," she said, waving at the tall structure painted with a winding black on white design. "The view up there is something else."

"We locals don't go doing stuff like that in the middle of summer," she said as she made a U-turn.

She drove across the bridge and turned right to take them past Castillo de San Marcos. The old fort, a huge structure built of coquina stone, had stood guard over the city for hundreds of years. Horse-drawn carriages were parked along the right side of the road, and she watched carefully in case one of them was about to pull out onto the road.

"This city has a history of violence," she said as she parked so that he could look up at the fort. "Matanzas Bay. *Matanzas* means blood. At the same time, it's supposed to have more churches than most cities."

A horse-drawn carriage passed on the road, and the driver waved at Tess. "That was my first part-time job," she told him. "I loved it."

"So that's where you learned to be a tour guide."

She gave him a brief smile. "Can't help but be one when you grow up here. I should warn you every relative you have will want to come visit you now that you live in Florida."

"No one to visit. Mom died two years ago and I was an only child."

"Father?"

"In the military," he said briefly. "We've never been close."

He sensed that she was curious, but she didn't press him. "You?"

"My mother died several years ago, and I never knew my dad. My only relative is my aunt. Her husband is Gordon Baxter. Have you met him yet?"

"He sat in on the interview with the chief." Logan hadn't been impressed with her uncle and was a little relieved the man wasn't a blood relation of Tess's.

She nodded. "He and the chief are tight."

They drove around for another hour, and she filled him in on crime statistics and insider information about the city.

"Dinner break?" She'd brought a sandwich, but now she didn't feel like returning to the station for it.

"Sounds good. You choose."

"Seafood?"

"Seafood sounds good."

"Place not too far from here has the best shrimp in the county."

"Okay."

"Just ignore all the tourist shtick. You know—the mermaid paintings. Nautical décor."

A few minutes later, they settled into a booth with tall glasses of sweet tea and smoked mullet dip before them.

Logan ignored the menu and let Tess's order of a dozen shrimp—fried—and sides of cole slaw and French fries guide him.

"And hush puppies?" the waitress asked him.

Tess groaned.

"Problem?" Logan asked.

"No," said Tess.

Pam laughed. "I'll just bring you one. One can't hurt."

"I can't ever stop at one."

The waitress looked at Logan. "Guard your plate. Girl steals them right off it when you're not looking. Seen it too many times. Outright larceny." Chuckling, she left them to put in the order.

Logan took a sip of his tea. "So, Tess. Why'd you get into law enforcement?"

Her fingers tightened on her glass. She set it down. "Sam—my best friend, Samantha—was murdered my senior year in high school."

She traced the condensation on the side of her glass and frowned. "The killer's never been found."

2

They got a call just as they were finishing their Key lime pie.

"Okay, partner, let's roll," Tess said, rising from the table.

Logan pulled out his cell phone, aimed it at her, and snapped a photo before she had time to throw up her hands and stop him.

"Hey, what'd you do?"

"Just took a photo for posterity. It's our first case together," he said, getting into the passenger side of the car.

"What're you going to do, make a scrapbook?"

He chuckled. "Maybe."

She spared him a glance as they got in the car, and she flipped on the AC. "You're in a good mood."

"I'm always in a good mood."

"Oh, really?"

"Sure."

"We'll see."

"How can you not be in a good mood in a beautiful place like this?"

She drove down US 1 for a few miles.

"Well?"

"Well, what?"

"You didn't answer my question."

"I didn't realize it was a question. But I'll play your game. Yeah, it's hard not to be in a good mood in a beautiful place like this. But just because it's sunny Florida and there are a bunch of tourists running around on vacation doesn't mean that we don't have crime or problems."

"I know. I'm a cop, remember?"

She nodded and stopped at a red light. When she heard the driver of the car beside her rev his engine, she looked over at him.

"Wanna race, baby?" the guy called over and revved his engine again.

"Probably not a good idea. There might be a cop around."

"Nah, I'm good at spotting cops."

Tess just smiled, held up her ID, and tried not to laugh when his jaw dropped.

"Aw, man," he said and when the light changed, he moved forward with the speed of an old lady.

"Killjoy," said Logan.

She drove on. "Where we're going might ruin your day, too."

"How? This is the first case we get to work together. I'm looking forward it."

"Why'd you move here?"

He shrugged. "Looking for a change of pace."

She knew from reading up on him that he'd cracked some big cases in Chicago. One of these days she'd find out why he'd moved here.

"Well, here's our big B & E investigation," she announced.

She pulled into the driveway of a small concrete block house painted bright flamingo pink. The yard was covered with every lawn ornament imaginable: plaster religious statues, plastic geese dressed in clothes, whirligig flowers, and more.

Tess had been just as agog when she'd seen the house the first time.

An elderly lady with frizzy scarlet hair opened the door. She wore a purple caftan and a cat draped around her neck.

"Why Tess, I wasn't expecting you!" the woman exclaimed. "Why aren't you wearing your uniform?"

"I'm a detective now, Mrs. Ramsey. This is my partner, Logan McMillan."

The woman's penciled eyebrows rose as she looked him over. "Good to meet you, Detective."

"We're here to investigate the break-in you reported, Mrs. Ramsey."

"Come in, come in," she said, opening the door a few more inches. "Watch out. Don't want to let anyone out."

"Anyone?" Logan murmured beside Tess.

"Watch your ankles," she hissed, looking around.

"I put Cammy up," Mrs. Ramsey said.

"Thank you." Tess pulled her notepad from her pocket. "You said someone broke in the back door last night. Can we check it out?"

"You know the way, dear."

Mrs. Ramsey settled back down onto the sofa and turned the volume up louder on the television. "Diamonique Hour is on QVC."

Tess led the way through the living room and into the kitchen. Several cats were lying in the sink. Another couple peered down from their post on the top of the refrigerator. She checked the back door, looking for signs of forced entry and finding none. Dutifully she went through the rest of the house with Logan.

When he shot her a puzzled look, she nodded, put her finger to her lips, and returned to the living room.

"Mrs. Ramsey?"

The woman tore her gaze from the television. "Will you look at that! Lovely bridal set, isn't it? I always liked the emerald cut. Makes even a small diamond look big." She tilted her head and studied Logan. "Are you married?"

He looked startled. "Uh, no, ma'am."

She nodded, then raised her eyebrows at Tess. "I see."

Tess wanted to roll her eyes. "Mrs. Ramsey, we didn't find any sign of a break-in. We checked all your doors and windows."

"Well, I suppose that's all well and good. But where's my diamond necklace?"

"Show me where you last saw it."

She lifted the cat on her lap and set it down on the sofa, then hauled herself to her feet. "Same place as always. Keep my jewelry box in the armoire in the master bedroom, under my shapewear." She shot a look at Logan. "They don't call them girdles anymore."

Tess nearly choked at Logan's expression.

"I—didn't know that."

"We'll be right back," Tess said.

"I'll be here."

"Nice young man," Mrs. Ramsey told her. "Single, huh?"

This time Tess did roll her eyes.

And got the look. The teacher look.

She straightened. "Uh, yes, ma'am."

Mrs. Ramsey opened the door to the master bedroom, and a huge white cat shot out of the room.

"Cat incoming!" she yelled to Logan and held her breath. When she didn't hear anything, she let it out.

"See? It's not here!" Mrs. Ramsey said, holding an empty jewelry case.

Tess nodded. "Description?" she asked and made notes in her pad as the woman rattled off the details that Tess knew by heart: Husband gave to her for their first anniversary. One carat. Oval shape. Platinum setting and chain. Irreplaceable.

She closed the pad with a snap. "We'll do our best to find out who took it."

They walked back into the living room. Tess wondered if she'd find Logan writhing in pain. Instead, Cujo—er, Cammy—looked adoringly at Logan as he scratched her head.

"Nice cat," he told Mrs. Ramsey.

She beamed. "Thank you. I always say Cammy knows a good person." She turned to Tess. "I'm glad you didn't bring that Smithers man. Cammy doesn't like him. Or that husband of your aunt's." She made a face. "Never liked him."

"Smithers?"

"Your uncle. Always seemed . . . sneaky. You know? I could never prove—" she stopped.

"Never could prove what?" Tess asked, trying to look casual. "I won't say anything."

Mrs. Ramsey sighed. "I could never prove he cheated on tests in my class. But I know he did." She glanced at Logan. "I taught long enough I had Tess's uncle *and* Tess in my classes at the high school."

"How about that?"

"We have to go, Mrs. Ramsey. I'll call you if we find your necklace. In the meantime, be sure to keep the doors and windows locked."

"I will, dear. And you promise you'll read a book this week."

"I will."

"Thanks for warning me about the cat."

"I got your back." She glanced over when he didn't say anything. "Cat got your tongue?"

"Thought women didn't crack jokes like that."

She shrugged. "Couldn't resist. You want to stop for something to drink? I know a place that has great sweet tea."

"You Southerners sure like your iced tea."

"Sweet tea."

She got the tea and a big cookie called a sand tart. Logan didn't eat sweets much but she hadn't steered him wrong in what she'd chosen to eat at their break. As usual, she introduced him to the woman behind the counter. He knew from his years as a beat cop you got to know your neighborhood, but it seemed like Tess knew everyone.

They settled in a big booth and watched the tourists walking around sweating in the afternoon heat. Now and then, a few of them straggled inside, sighed over the air conditioning, and ordered drinks and pastries.

"So tell me about Mrs. Ramsey. She seems . . . quite a character."

"She wasn't always like this. She was my high school English teacher for several years. Got bumped up when I did. I thought it was a coincidence at the time, but now I know better."

"What do you mean?" He took a bite of the cookie and nearly groaned it was so good.

She shrugged. "Things happen for a reason. I learned a lot from her but not just about English. She really helped me after—after Sam died."

Logan took a sip of the tea and found it a bit sweet for his taste. "So how long has she been thinking someone's breaking into her house and stealing her jewelry?"

Tess lifted a hand when someone walked past and greeted her. It was turning out this was a smaller town than he'd originally thought.

"About a year now. Her husband died not long after Sam, and it took a lot out of her." She set the cookie down, half-eaten, and looked up at him. "She hasn't been . . . eccentric until recently. So far it seems harmless, but I'm going to keep an eye on her."

She sat back. "I guess this is different for you, coming from the big city."

"Big city's made up of small neighborhoods," he said. "You gonna eat that cookie?"

"Help yourself."

He bit into it and then realized it made him think about her lips had touched the same place his were doing now. Don't go there, he warned himself. You're partners. Not a good idea to mix personal and work.

Their break was short-lived. They'd barely finished the tea when they got a call to investigate several more break-ins—real this time.

"Not a lot of excitement since you've been here," she said as they got into the car after the last one.

"Fine by me," he said. "I'm not looking for excitement."

She looked at him, started to say something, and then started the car.

"What?"

"Nothing."

"Might as well ask. It's the only way we'll get to know each other."

"What makes you think I want to know about you?"

He laughed and gazed out at the car window. "Of course you do. The reason both of us wanted to be detectives is because

27

we're hypercurious." He looked back at her. "And the more we know about each other, the better we'll work together."

He watched her as she stopped at a red light and glanced around. "Then there's safety, too. Being a detective is less dangerous than being a patrol officer. But if there's a situation, good partners who know and trust each other can up the odds of surviving it."

"Well, things are pretty quiet here," she told him as she turned off the ignition and unclipped her seat belt. "Being attacked by Cammy is probably as hazardous as things are going to get."

Logan remembered the way the cat had come tearing out the bedroom toward him. He'd had a few uncomfortable moments until it got closer and he saw it didn't have a crazed look on its face. Trusting, he bent and scratched its head, and everything was fine.

He didn't have to wonder why it had attacked Smithers. Seemed to him that the cat had good judgment there. He didn't care for Smithers talking about Tess the way he had and was glad he'd gotten her for a partner.

"So, got big plans for the weekend?" he asked.

"Some real exciting stuff. A few home repairs, church on Sunday."

"I like to do home repairs."

She reached into her pocket for the cards she carried and handed him one. "You're welcome to attend if you like."

"Oh, this is for your church."

Her lips quirked in a grin. "Yeah. I do my own home repairs. Why don't you buy your own place so you can have some fun?"

He fingered the card before putting in his own pocket. "I'm renting until I know what part of the city I want to live in."

"Smart."

He met her eyes. "Yeah. I thought so. Maybe you can give me some advice on where I should buy."

"Sure. Take some time. Not everyone likes living here."

"I'm liking it fine," he said, pausing on the sidewalk to look around. He looked back at her. "I'm liking it just fine."

3

They could talk all they wanted about fancy cures for stress. Tess felt it slip from her shoulders when she ran on the beach. Or when she walked into the quilt shop her aunt co-owned with a friend.

Claudia looked up from the quilt she was sewing on a frame with Muriel and Paula.

"Good morning! I didn't expect you after you said your shift changed."

Tess bent and hugged her, then sat down and nodded at the other women. "Day off."

"You just missed your aunt. She was in this morning after they discharged her from the hospital, but she's taking the afternoon off."

"I'm sorry I missed her. I'll give her a call later. She doing okay?"

"Doing fine."

Tess said hello to everyone and felt herself relaxing. She pulled her quilt from her tote bag, threaded a needle, and began sewing. The quilt shop had become one of her favorite places. She could relax here like she couldn't seem to relax lately. It seemed like she worked so much, and when she went home she knew she needed to relax but couldn't. There was always something to do: housework, a DIY project—she'd bought a fixer-upper. Another look over Sam's case.

Enough already.

Here in the little shop crowded with colorful fabrics and threads and yarn, she could just sit and work on something creative and let her mind wander.

The quilt pattern was something different for her—a mariner's quilt. She'd always liked this pattern. She'd grown up near water and watched the sailboats from the shore. When she'd flipped through the big quilt pattern book looking for her next quilt, she'd fallen in love with it.

"Tell us about your new job," Claudia invited, looking at Tess over her cat's-eye reading glasses.

"Yes, do tell," Donna said, her grin full of mischief.

"And don't tell us you can't talk about it because it's work," Monica told her.

Tess shook her head and laughed. "You sound like a bunch of high school girls."

Claudia fluffed her hair. "Well, some of us aren't far from that time."

Monica guffawed. "We're ALL decades from that, honey. Kathy might get away with pretending she's still the young local beauty queen, but the rest of us aren't getting away with it."

"I'm glad she's home," Tess said.

"Don't go trying to change the subject, darling," Claudia advised. "I already let everyone know how Kathy is doing. Give us the scoop on your new job. And especially your new partner."

Tess stopped sewing. "How do you know about my new partner?"

"Oh, honey, you aren't the only one who can find things out," Claudia told her.

"You've been prying information out of my aunt." Tess tried to look stern but knew she failed when Claudia just chuckled.

"So, dish," Claudia urged.

Tess shook her head. "Nothing much to say. We've only worked together for one day. He seems okay."

Claudia snorted, then looked at the other women. "'Okay.' *Right.* I hear he's gorgeous. And more important, single."

"I don't think you got that information from my aunt." Tess concentrated on her stitching. She looked up. "Or my uncle."

"I have a mole in the police department," Claudia admitted. "She told me this Logan is cute and the two of you looked like a good match."

"We're partners," Tess said. "How are women ever going to be looked at as professionals as long as people only see us as looking for romantic hookups?"

"She's right," Monica spoke up. "We shouldn't tease Tess. She worked hard for this opportunity. Police work is still a man's world, even here in our small town."

"Especially in our small town," Tess muttered. She parked her needle in the quilt and stood. "Is there any coffee?"

"Just made a fresh pot," Claudia said.

"See, you made her feel uncomfortable," she heard Monica say behind her.

"C'mon, Tess can take it. Like you said, she's been working in a man's world for a long time."

"But we're women," Donna could be heard to say. "We should be supportive."

"We're being supportive. We want her to be happy."

"Well, I'm not sure she appreciates us playing matchmaker."

Tess stood out of sight and grinned as she sipped her coffee. They meant well. Trouble was, everyone thought they knew what was best for you.

She gave it a couple of minutes and then walked back into the room. Before she sat again, though, she went to the front window and looked out. She'd been so determined to make detective she hadn't thought she'd miss her old job. But she did. She missed the contact that she had with the residents, the visitors.

Returning to her seat, she set her coffee on a nearby table and resumed sewing. Peace settled back over her. She quilted at home but the weekly class had become a fun way to be with other women interested in the same thing. They were a mixed group of ages and interests and different levels of skill in quilting. Her aunt and Claudia were the longtime quilters, Tess had been quilting for about four years, and Donna and Monica had joined the class earlier in the summer.

Her aunt had gotten her interested in quilting but Tess doubted she'd have grown and stretched as much without the class. Each time she finished a quilt, the other women had joined her aunt in convincing Tess to try more complicated patterns.

She looked around the shop again. It had become like a second home to her, a place to feel comfortable and be herself.

Logan surveyed the boxes piled in the kitchen and sighed.

The last thing he wanted to do was unpack on a beautiful Saturday morning. On the other hand, he hadn't made much progress so far.

Tess had said she was going to do some home repair this weekend. That sounded like a lot more fun than unpacking to him. Too bad she hadn't let him help her. He considered hanging around the local big box hardware store, but he had no idea if there was more than one in the town . . . and who knew how many hardware stores she could be visiting.

Resigned, he unpacked the boxes of glasses and plates and arranged them in cupboards he'd scrubbed earlier in the week. The kitchen was as dated as the house. The funny little World War II bungalow reminded him of his grandmother's when he saw it, and it was close to work. Besides, he'd told himself he didn't have time to look for something to buy. Later, when he felt settled in the job and knew the area better, he'd get a realtor to help him find a place.

Pots and pans were next, the few cookbooks he owned, and the few staples that had been worth moving. He'd have to grocery shop today or tomorrow if he didn't want to live on takeout the following week. He wasn't that great a cook, but he knew living on takeout wasn't good for anyone.

Linens and towels were next, then a couple boxes of books. A box of shoes—he owned more running shoes than dress shoes—followed.

The stack of empty boxes by the front door grew. When his stomach growled, he looked at the time and was surprised that he'd been working so long. He checked the fridge knowing it was a futile effort. How could there be anything in there when he hadn't shopped?

So he started carrying the boxes out. After the last one, he locked up the house and started out to the car to go get a sandwich.

That's when he saw the gray and white striped cat lying on the roof of his car parked in the carport. At first, he figured it was enjoying the shade but then as he got closer, he saw the blood on its head. It moaned piteously.

"Wow, looks like you got into a fight," he said, approaching cautiously. He didn't want to get bitten or scratched.

He saw his neighbor working in his flower bed. "Hey, Kyle, this your cat?"

The man looked up and wiped at the sweat running down his face. "Nah. It's hung around the neighborhood for about a year. Wife feeds it sometimes when it comes around. Told her no more cats in the house."

"Looks hurt."

"I heard cats fighting last night." He got to his feet and walked over to the fence separating their yards. "Ouch."

"I think he needs stitches."

Kyle glanced back at his house, then back at Logan. "Chase it away. Last thing I need is for Nancy to want to take it to the vet. Can't afford the ones we have."

The cat moaned again. Logan didn't have the heart to chase it away. "You got a carrier I can borrow?"

"Yeah, I'll get it."

Kyle moved faster than Logan expected him to. Probably was feeling happy someone else was going to be paying this bill.

Logan pulled out his cell and hit speed dial. "Hey, Tess, you know a good vet? One that treats cats?"

"I didn't know you had a cat."

"Don't. It's a stray. Needs a vet."

She gave him the number. "Thanks. Talk to you later."

Kyle returned with the carrier, his wife trailing behind him. "Logan's gonna take him to the vet," he said to her. "It's not our problem."

"I know," she said, frowning at him. She looked at Logan. "This is really nice of you."

Logan shrugged. "He needs to be seen. Then maybe the vet can find him a good home."

He took the carrier from Kyle and opened the door on it. Then he approached the cat. "Okay, nice kitty. C'mon, get in the carrier."

The cat just looked at him. Logan could swear it was a look of disdain. His mother's cat always did that.

He moved closer, and the cat rose and began backing away. "Kyle, maybe you can help me? Get on the other side of the car so he can't go that way?"

Looking wary, Kyle moved to the other side of the car. "I'm not gonna wrestle him. Last thing I need is to get scratched."

Logan set the carrier on the hood of the car and began edging toward the cat, talking in a low and soothing tone just as he might do if he had a jumper. The cat backed up and started to slide off the roof. Kyle lunged for him, but when he touched its flanks the cat turned and hissed at him. Kyle backed off, nearly tripping over his own feet.

Taking advantage of the cat being distracted, Logan lunged for it but got a swipe of a paw for his trouble.

"Guys, guys!" Nancy said with a big sigh. "Let me try." She walked up to the cat. "C'mon, Joe, come to Nancy, there's a good Joe."

"Joe?"

She shrugged. "Looks like a Joe to me." She turned her attention to the cat. "Poor baby, don't you worry about these guys, they just want to help. Let's get you in the crate and get a doctor to help you feel better. C'mon, sweetie pie."

And the cat walked toward her and let her pick it up and put it in the crate.

Nancy fastened the door and turned to smile at Logan. "There you go. What vet you taking him to?"

When he told her, she nodded. "Good one. I've used her before." She turned to her husband. "C'mon, I'll fix you a cold drink, and then you can get back to weeding."

"Lucky me," Kyle said and followed her back into their yard.

Logan loaded the carrier in the car and backed out of the drive. This wasn't the way he'd thought he'd spend his day off, but it wouldn't take long to take it to the vet and leave it for treatment.

The vet turned out to be a pretty woman in her thirties who competently stitched up Joe's head all the while she conducted an interrogation of Logan that ranked up there with some of the best he'd witnessed in his line of work. So he knew Tess? Where had he come from? How did he like St. Augustine? And the inevitable, how did his wife feel about it?

His response that he wasn't married led to lifted eyebrows and a nod. "So you two are single?"

"Yeah. But he's not mine, he's a neighborhood stray. I was hoping you could help him find a home."

"I'll be happy to post his photo on the bulletin board at the reception window," she said. "But first, we need to get this guy neutered. I'll give you a discount seeing as you're a police officer."

"Oh. Okay." He winced a little at the price she quoted, but nodded.

"Bring him back Monday. You'll need to keep him indoors while his head heals and make sure he doesn't take off."

This was getting better and better. Resigned, he let her load the cat into the carrier and stopped at the reception window to pay the bill. His wallet a little lighter, he returned home and set the carrier in the middle of the living room. Now what?

He opened the door and Joe just sat inside it, glaring at him. Shrugging, he went into the kitchen, filled a bowl with water and returned to the living room. "There you go. You have to be thirsty by now."

He might need other things, too. Pocketing his keys, he let himself out of the house and walked over to Kyle and Nancy's.

"I came to borrow something," he said when she opened the door. "I was hoping you had some kitty litter you could spare until I go to the store?"

He returned home with half a bag of litter, some dry kibble, two cans of cat food, and an offer to look in on the cat whenever needed.

His cell phone rang. Tess's name and number came up on the display. "Cat came through it fine," he said before she could speak.

"That's nice, but that's not why I called," she said tersely. "We have a homicide."

4

How many homicides have you investigated?"

"This is my first official one," Tess said. "But I've been on scene for about a half a dozen through the years. Why, are you worried I can't carry my weight?"

The minute the words were out, she heard the defensiveness in them and wanted to bite her tongue. Oh well, better she said it than held it inside.

"Not at all. Some places a detective doesn't see one for years before they have to investigate one."

Tess forced herself to relax her fingers on the steering wheel. "And other places like Chicago you see lots of them, right?"

"That's not what I'm saying. But I have to say I'm sorry to have seen a good share." He slipped on his sunglasses. "I read the statistics before I took the job. Some years you don't have one here."

"Did you come here because of that?"

"No."

Just "no." Talk about a man of few words.

They drove in silence for a few miles, and then Tess took a left turn and parked behind two patrol cars. One of the officers was already stringing crime scene tape around the porch of a small home.

Tess and Logan ducked under the tape. They slipped paper booties over their shoes while another officer filled them in on what they knew so far.

"Victim's Antonia Sanchez, twenty-one. Worked as a legal assistant at Colbert and Colbert. M.E.'s with the victim in the living room. We're working on notifying family."

They entered the house and Tess stood there for a moment, frowning. Something seemed so familiar.

"What is it?"

She looked at Logan, then around the room. "I—I don't know. I've been here before." Shaking her head, she continued into the living room.

A woman's body lay sprawled in the middle of the room, dark red blood pooling on the carpet around her head. Philip, the medical examiner, glanced up at Tess and Logan and nodded. "I'd say she's been dead for twenty-four hours. Blunt force trauma to the head as you can see."

Tess stared at her face. The woman was young—in her twenties. She was pretty, with long brown hair, her slim figure dressed in a pink t-shirt and jeans. Her blue eyes stared sightlessly at the ceiling. She wore an expensive-looking gold chain at her neck, and her fingers were adorned with several rings set with small gemstones.

"It wasn't a robbery," the M.E. said, pointing at the jewelry.

"Rape?" she asked, noticing the way the victim's jeans were unsnapped and her shirt was half-tucked into the waistband.

He nodded. "I'll do the usual tests when I get her back to the morgue."

"I know her. I came to a party here once. A baby shower for her sister Maria who works in Records. Maria called her Toni."

"Do you need to step outside for a few minutes?" Logan asked quietly at her side.

She took a deep breath and shook her head. "No. It's bound to happen when you live in a small town and you've lived here since birth."

"Tell me about it," the medical examiner said, his expression hangdog. "I've been at this for twenty years and I've seen way too many friends and acquaintances in my morgue."

Tess took notes as the M.E. made his usual methodical exam of the body, and she asked him question after question. Logan observed and said little. The crime scene team went over the house looking for evidence, and the photographer bent close to record the body from every angle.

Then the M.E. moved Toni's head and Tess's breath caught. She'd seen that mark on the skin of the nape before. . . . It was engraved on her memory forever.

"He's back," she whispered. As the room and the noises around her receded, she felt like she was being pulled into a tunnel.

"Tess! Snap out of it!" Logan was saying as he shook her arm.

"I'm okay." She shook her head and forced herself back to the present. "Phil, that's the mark we've seen on three homicides now. The first one was on my friend, remember?"

He nodded. "I'll check it against a photo back at the morgue, but like you, I've seen it enough now to recognize it. I was hoping this guy was dead or in prison for another crime." He looked up at the photographer. "Get some shots of this."

That done, he encased the woman's hands in plastic evidence bags. "Let's hope we get lucky this time and she has some skin cells from the perp under her fingernails."

43

"Tess, there's no evidence of a break-in," Jason, one of the team reported when he walked into the room. "I'm thinking she knew the perp, let him in."

She jerked her head at a commotion at the door. The officer guarding the door was trying to keep Maria from entering the house.

"What's happened? Is Toni hurt? You have to let me see her!"

Tess strode to the door and led Maria outside onto the porch. Tears streaked the woman's face.

"One of the clerks came to tell me she heard the call come in and recognized the address. What's happened? You have to tell me, Tess!"

She gently pushed Maria down to sit on the porch swing and sat beside her. It wasn't the first time she'd had to do a death notification; it wouldn't be the last.

"I'm so sorry, Maria. She's dead."

"No," Maria said, shaking her head. "I was just with her last night. She can't be. I want to see her."

Tess hesitated. There was no one solution, no one right way to handle this. It had been the worst day of her life when she'd seen Sam carried out in a body bag.

"I want to see her," Maria insisted. She burst into tears, sobbing hysterically in Tess's arms. She let her cry until Phil came to the door.

Tess tried not to tense up, but Maria must have felt it. She sat back and found a tissue in her pocket to wipe at her tears. "What is it?" She looked over at the door and saw Phil.

"Hi."

"I'm so sorry, Maria. Do you want to see Toni before we leave?"

Tess could feel Maria trembling just sitting next to her. Maria nodded. "Thank you."

He came forward and took her hand and when Maria stood, she reached back for Tess's hand.

Together they walked inside and Tess watched Maria make the formal identification of the body. Maria let out a keening wail when she saw her sister and for a moment she sagged, and Phil and Tess had to hold her up. And then she nodded and turned to Tess.

"Get me out of here," she told Tess. "I want out of here."

Just as Tess turned to do as she asked, Logan stepped forward. "Maria, I'm sorry for your loss, but can you stay here for a few minutes? Help us?"

Tess rounded on him. "How can you ask her that now?"

⸎

Logan looked at Tess. He saw the pain and sorrow of today. But there was more in those stormy gray eyes flashing at him. In them, he could read remembered horror from her friend Samantha's death.

"We need to do this," he said quietly. "You more than anyone know that."

He watched her close her eyes, then open them. She sighed. "I know."

"Can you think of anyone—anyone at all who might have wanted to hurt Toni?" he asked. "Did she have a boyfriend? Was there any trouble at work that she mentioned?"

Maria shook her head. "Everyone loved Toni, and she didn't have boyfriend trouble. He's overseas, doing his last tour in Afghanistan. They were hoping to get—" she stopped, fought for control. "They were hoping to get married."

Logan stepped closer and waited until she lifted her eyes to meet his. "Maria, do you think you can look at Toni and tell me if there's anything that looks different about her. Something

45

that doesn't look right. Anything missing? I know I'm asking a lot."

Maria glanced at Tess when she moved to slip her arm around her waist. "I can do this. It's okay. Really. I want the monster who killed my Toni caught."

Logan watched her take a deep breath and seem to steel herself to look at her sister.

"Take your time. Don't force anything."

He glanced at Tess, and she nodded. They both knew why he asked Maria to do this. Sometimes the killer took something as a trophy. Rearranged her hair or altered her clothing. Posed her in a way meant to send a message—often obscene. He was grateful at least this time, the perp hadn't done that. Snuffing out the life of a beautiful young woman with her life ahead of her had been bad enough.

"One of her rings is missing," Maria said finally. "It was just a little birthstone ring I gave her. A little sapphire. Not worth much. I couldn't afford much of a stone. I gave it to her for her *quinceañera*."

"Good," Logan told her quietly. "This is very helpful Maria. Can you see anything else? You know her better than anyone else."

"Except our mother," Maria said and tears began running down her cheeks again. "Oh, I'm glad our mother isn't here to see this."

Tess gave her a reassuring squeeze. "She's welcoming Toni into heaven," she murmured.

Maria nodded and wiped away her tears. She frowned. "Toni loved wearing her jewelry. We didn't have money for it years ago, so when she started working she'd treat herself to a piece every so often. Maybe we should look in her jewelry box."

"Good idea. And keep looking around as we walk to it." Tess kept her arm around her waist.

A single glass sat on the counter next to the sink. A crime scene tech looked up from his examination of the floor. "I dusted that for prints. I doubt the perp was stupid enough to drink from it and leave his DNA, but you never know."

Logan nodded and gave the room another visual sweep.

"Nothing's off in here," Maria said. "Toni was such a good housekeeper, kept everything so clean."

They moved on to the master bedroom where Maria put on a pair of gloves Logan handed her and went through her sister's jewelry box. "I don't think anything's missing."

"Excuse me for a moment," Tess said.

Logan let Maria move from room to room without prompting her. She looked shell-shocked, moving on auto-pilot, but appeared determined to help them. But he knew he would need to draw this to a close very soon before she simply crashed.

The medical examiner appeared in the doorway, signaled Logan that he was leaving. Logan nodded and was glad that Maria didn't notice their nonverbal communication. The last thing she needed was to see her sister being zipped into a body bag and carried out.

Tess had witnessed it, though. Logan could tell how it had affected her and wished he could have spared her. When she saw him watching her, she met his gaze, lifted her chin, and almost seemed to draw herself up, all business.

"Maria, I was just wondering. Where's Paco?"

The woman clapped her hand to her mouth. "Oh my! That's what's wrong. Where's Paco?"

"A dog?" Logan asked.

"Chihuahua." Maria began calling its name as she went to the back yard. Logan and Tess followed.

The dog was nowhere to be found.

Tess dialed Animal Control, but no Chihuahua had been brought in by their staff or the public. She relayed a description of the dog and left Maria's phone number in case anyone saw Paco.

Logan made a note to ask that the officers doing a neighborhood canvas find out if anyone had seen the dog or heard it barking around the time of the murder.

An officer appeared in the doorway, and Tess walked over to him. They talked briefly, and then Tess returned to Maria's side. "Your husband is here to take you home, Maria. I called him. Father Angelo is on his way to meet both of you at your house."

She led Maria to the front door, walking her quickly past the place where Toni had lain.

Logan watched the man who wrapped his arms around Maria and led her to a car.

"Husband?"

Tess nodded. She turned to him. "What are you thinking?"

"Hmm?"

"Something's on your mind."

"The dog," he said. "Chihuahuas are fiercely protective of their owners. My mother got one after I went off to college, and I got bitten more than once when I went home for the holidays. I don't know how someone got in with Paco here."

He watched her rub her forehead. "When's the last time you ate?"

"I'm fine."

"I'm sure you are," he said. "But that's not what I asked. All I've had today is a chicken sandwich on my way to the vet early this morning. I say we take a break, get some food, and compare notes." He closed his notebook, shoved it in the back pocket of his jeans, and strode out of the room.

She caught up with him at the car and tossed him the keys. "You drive. I want to look something up."

He slid into the driver's seat and had to adjust the seat only a little—she was nearly as tall as he was. She got in the passenger side, buckled up, then immediately became engrossed surfing the Internet on her cell phone.

"Where do you want to eat?" he asked.

"You pick."

"How's that Greek place near the station? Good?"

She nodded.

He drove there, parked, and waited. It took her several minutes before she looked up and around.

"Let's get inside and order," he said. "Then you can tell me about your friend's case."

5

Her name was Samantha Marshall," she began. "She was eighteen and the first victim of a serial killer who has since murdered four more young women about the same age."

He stopped her by touching her hand lying on top of the table. "I'm sorry. I didn't say that well. Tell me about your friend, Tess."

Tess stared at his hand covering hers and then lifted her gaze to his. She saw compassion, not pity in his eyes.

"I called her Sam," she said. "We grew up together, in the same neighborhood. Went to the same school. Double-dated. She was a tomboy, and there wasn't a sport she couldn't play. She won a scholarship to U of F—University of Florida. We were going to go off to college, be roommates—until she got killed."

She stared off into the distance. "It was the night of the prom. We'd gone to dinner before with the Johnson boys—we were seeing twin brothers. She thought that was funny—we were so alike we could have been twins, and we were dating them. Sometimes life is stranger than fiction."

The waitress brought their meals, but she let hers sit as she remembered. "I left the dance because Jimmy couldn't seem to

51

keep his hands to himself. He kept saying he hoped he'd get lucky that night." She blushed. "I asked myself what I'd seen in him. He was cute, but he was so crude, so selfish."

"He was a teenaged guy," Logan said. His mouth quirked in a grin. "I'm not sure I was way more mature at that age."

"I'm sure you were a *lot* more mature than Jimmy. Anyway, I stomped out of the place they were having the prom and then realized I should have told Sam I was catching a cab home. But I couldn't find her. Turned out she'd gone looking for me after she heard the brothers talking, and Jimmy admitted he'd been a jerk.

"The three of us went looking for her. We spent hours going every place we could think of. Mrs. Ramsey went with us. You know, the cat lady who couldn't find her necklace the other day? She was a chaperone at the prom. So she and her husband joined the search. It was so not like Sam to go off without saying something."

She took a sip of her sweet tea. Her throat suddenly felt so dry. "Finally, we all went home. They found Sam the next day in the park near the lighthouse."

Tess looked at him. "It was so ironic. She loved that lighthouse, even worked part-time in the gift shop."

"You and Phil said Toni had the same mark today as Sam."

"Yeah." She pulled out her cell phone and called up the image. "See, it's the same as Toni's."

"Could it be a copycat?"

"I don't think so. We've never released that detail to the public."

He studied it. "Any speculation on what it means?"

She shook her head. "Everyone just thinks it's a letter M. But of course it means more than that to the killer."

The waitress stopped by their table. "Something wrong with the food?"

"No, Kim, I'm sure it's fine." Tess picked up her fork and began eating. "I was just telling Logan here about Sam."

"The two of them used to come in here after school with some friends," Kim told Logan. "I was just out of high school and starting waitressing."

Tess smiled. "We used to order cherry Cokes and French fries."

"One of the other girls got jealous," Kim said. "She was this little rich girl, daddy was a doctor. Wanted to know why Tess and Sam used to get a bigger plate of French fries than she did. I told her it was because they shared."

She sighed. "Gotta go see what old man Roberts wants now. Let me know if you need anything."

"We shared because we were like sisters," Tess explained. "But we also shared because our families didn't have much money. My mom was a single parent, and Sam's dad was out of work a lot. We even shared prom dresses."

Logan's eyes narrowed. "She was wearing one you'd worn before?"

"Yes. And don't think I didn't feel guilty over that later. What if the killer had been targeting me? We know they often know their victims or they stalk them for a while."

He took a sip of his sweet tea. "Anything stick out about that night? Anyone leave the prom?"

She grinned. "Have you forgotten your prom night? It's all about the couples sneaking outside to make out."

"True. What I mean is, was there anything about the night that bothered you? Made you suspicious of anyone?"

Tess stirred her mashed potatoes. "Well, I remember that Gordon gave Wendell a lot of grief over where he was when Sam went missing. Gordon was working security. Anyway, Wendell had an alibi. He'd gotten into trouble for adding the contents of a flask he'd sneaked in and put into the punch bowl. The coach saw him and was going to send him home, but then I walked up to them and asked where Sam was."

"Finish eating and we'll go make a report to the shift supervisor, then pull the files on the previous vics and start looking at them."

She wasn't really in the mood to eat but who knew when they'd take time again to eat. And she hadn't been able to shop earlier today, as she'd intended.

Kim came to refill their tea and then returned to offer Logan dessert. He chose the apple pie she said was fresh baked.

When Kim turned to leave, he stopped her. "Tess, aren't you having anything?"

"Oh, I know what she's having," the waitress told him breezily. "She can't resist our baklava."

Tess made a face at the woman's back, then laughed, and shook her head. "She thinks she knows me so well."

"I guess that's the blessing—and the curse of small towns, eh?"

"You're right," she said. "You're so right." Then she frowned. "What?"

"Well, it's obvious, isn't it? The killer is one of us. He's lived here all this time, walked among us. Maybe gone to the same schools, the same beach, eaten at the same restaurants."

She smiled as Kim placed the Greek pastry in front of her. "Knows us well."

"Huh?" said Kim.

"Nothing. Just thinking out loud."

Kim grinned and made a circular motion with her head near her temple before she walked away.

"I'm not crazy," she said as she dug into the baklava, savoring the bite of the flaky pastry, honey, and almonds.

"No, you're not," he told her. "That's why he's been hard to catch. He's been able to blend right in and not call attention to himself. But the thing about serial killers is that they think they're smarter than everyone else. Sometimes they get arrogant and slip up."

He smiled, an almost . . . feral smile. "We're going to get him, Tess. Count on it."

Tess had learned to count on herself and no one else. She didn't know Logan McMillan well yet. But she had the feeling she could count on what he said.

———— ✎ ————

Talk about a challenge.

Logan liked one although he sure hadn't wanted it to come about this way. So, this seemingly quaint historic city with the people he'd found so friendly—harbored a serial killer . . .

Well, no one should have been surprised, he guessed. The city had a violent past—five countries had sent soldiers great distances to kill for it and claim it for the crown. Five countries had flown their flag. Five countries had spilled blood to grasp a city and state that was an entrance to the continent and untold riches.

When Tess had shown him around the first day, he'd started to tell her that he'd visited it for vacations several times. Then he'd decided to stay silent so he could see the city through her eyes. And see something of who and what she was in the showing him around.

So far they'd worked well even with their differing styles— how *did* the woman think of so many questions when she was talking to the M.E.? Granted, asking questions showed a quick and agile mind, and there was a steep learning curve to being a detective. He'd been on the job longer than she had, but not so long that he didn't remember being just like her when he started.

And since he was the new guy in town and didn't have the advantage of knowing the details of the past murders, he was going to be the one asking a lot of questions.

He looked over and was sorry he did. Tess seemed to be deriving a great deal of pleasure in licking the honey from her fork. She set it down and sighed.

Kim slapped the check down on the table and shook her head. "You'll just hate yourself if you have a second piece."

"I know."

Logan reached for the check. "My treat," he said when she asked what her share was. "I have a feeling I'm going to be very glad that you introduced me to this place."

"Yeah, well, you might not thank me if you get as addicted to that apple pie as I have to their baklava."

"True."

She grinned. It was nice to see her face light up after the stress and sadness earlier.

Logan got his change, left a tip for Kim on the table, and followed Tess out to the car. The heat hadn't let up. He was afraid to ask just when it started getting cooler in these parts.

"Chief wants to see the two of you," his assistant said when they walked into the station.

They exchanged a glance and changed direction to head to his office. Jeremy Wallace was talking on the phone, but gestured for them to enter. Tess closed the door behind them and took the chair closest to Wallace's desk.

He hung up and looked at them. "Phil says our friend is back."

"Perp left his mark in the usual place," Tess said.

"Is it possible we have a copycat?" Wallace leaned back in his chair and steepled his fingers.

"Anything's possible, but no, I don't think so. The mark he left has never been revealed to the press."

"Both of you be back here at 0800 for a briefing." He flicked a glance at Logan, then studied Tess. "Big case your first week as a detective."

"Yes sir. I've done nothing but get ready for this for years."

He nodded. "Gordon thinks you can handle it. Says you've obsessed about trying to solve your friend's murder."

"Sometimes it takes obsessiveness."

"True." He turned his attention to Logan. "I want to catch this guy and lock him away for good. Maybe having some fresh eyes'll help."

"I hope so."

The phone rang. He picked it up and snapped, "I said no calls." He listened and muttered under his breath. "Tell him I'll call him back in five. No, don't let him try to bulldoze you. Tell him five minutes and hang up."

He slammed the phone down. "Press got wind. You two make yourselves scarce and don't say anything unless I tell you. Got it?"

"Yessir," they said in unison.

"Okay, briefing at 0800."

They were nearly out of the room when he barked, "I want your report on my desk pronto. Overtime's already authorized."

Logan followed Tess to their desks. "Let's get that report out of the way and then pull the files for all the cold cases. Four, right?"

"Right." She sat down and logged in on her computer. "Let's do this."

They worked well as a team even though they hadn't known each other long. Logan deferred to Tess sitting behind the computer and typing the report. Since he'd been a detective for longer than her, he knew more about doing them but her writing skills were better and, as she put it, his spelling was "atrocious." He'd reminded her he used a spell checker, but she'd dismissed that with a sniff. He couldn't argue that spell checkers stunk.

When the report was finished, she printed out a copy and handed it to Logan to deliver.

"Why not just send it to him?"

Tess shook her head. "Chief's a little old-fashioned. He wants to hold it in his hands. Give it to his assistant if she's there."

So Logan took the report and delivered it to the chief, then returned to find Tess had pulled a stack of files and set them on his desk.

"Just a little light reading, huh?"

Tess just made a noncommittal noise as she looked at something on her computer.

He sat down and opened the first file. The photo of a young woman lay on top. He studied it, aware that she'd looked up and was watching him. What must it have been like to see photos of her best friend like this? It couldn't compare to the first time he'd encountered a dead body on duty. He'd been lucky the victim had been a stranger.

"I made up a file of my own," she told him. "I can give you an overview."

He watched her body language. She lifted her chin—a tell that showed she was a little defensive. Someone had made her feel so. Smithers? So far she'd shown she was intelligent, methodical, and years ahead of others at her level of service. His gut told him she'd save him hours getting up to speed.

His gut had always stood him in good stead.

He nodded.

She pushed her chair around to the side of his desk and handed him a map. "Shows all the locations where the bodies were found."

"He started at the lighthouse, moved to the beach, then the fort, and a cemetery. Toni's different—she was killed at her house."

"That's different," she agreed. "But the killer does follow a pattern in the ages of his victims—they're all in their late teens or twenties. Pretty typical of serial killers."

She pulled out photos of the others and laid them on his desk. He found himself admiring her courage when she added one of her friend.

"Any pattern about time of year? Occupation? Any of them prostitutes?"

She gave him a level gaze. "You're not suggesting they're less worthy of having their murder solved because they were prostitutes?"

He met her gaze. "I know we haven't known each other long but do you really need to ask the question?"

Tess shook her head. "No. But I'm sorry to say that opinion isn't shared by everyone in the department."

"Judge not," he murmured.

"Anyway, to answer your questions, so far we haven't seen any pattern regarding timing—here's a chart to show when each occurred. Occupations have varied. Sam was a high school student; Carol, victim two, a nurse; Bobbi, a drug company rep; Susan, unemployed; Toni, a part-time college instructor and freelance writer."

He listened, took notes, and asked questions. When she ran down, he glanced at the clock and was surprised at how much time had passed.

"Guess we ought to knock off since we have to be back here in five hours," he said and wondered if she'd be able to back off and let it go for the night.

"I agree."

"I'm impressed with all the work you did," he said and meant it.

She began putting the items back into the master file—careful to organize them as meticulously as they'd been when she started. "Thanks. I learned from one of the best."

"The chief? Or your uncle?"

"My uncle. He saw I was interested in police work when I was in high school and he was a kind of mentor for me. I hung around their house a lot, joined Police Explorers. It was a logical thing to go after a criminal justice major once I graduated."

"Especially after you lost your friend."

She stood and walked over to lock the file in her desk. "Yeah."

Outside, the temperature had dropped quite a bit but the air still felt humid. The tourists were gone for the day, and there were few cars driving past.

"I'm starved. You?"

"I could eat."

"I don't suppose the diner's open?"

"No. But there's a good place not far from here. They'll even fix you fried potatoes since you're a Yankee."

He made a face. "I don't eat grits. Talk about tasteless."

She shook her head. "And here I thought you were a smart man."

6

Tess was dressed and out the door before 0700.

Logan was already at his desk when she got to the station.

He looked up. "Get any sleep?"

"Not much. You?" She set her coffee on her desk, sat down, and typed her password into her computer.

"Not much. Want a cat?"

"No. You have one to give away?"

"Free. With supplies. Free delivery. Oh, did I mention free?"

She laughed. "That doesn't sound good. You haven't had it long."

"Long enough," he said, leaning back and taking a sip of his own coffee. "He wanted to get out, so he howled and howled. I wasn't about to let him go fight another cat after I dropped a wad of cash at the vet's." He rubbed his forehead. "I'll get him back. He's getting neutered on Tuesday."

"So you're keeping him?" She gave her e-mail a quick scan.

"Only until I find him a home. At the least, if he gets out between now and then he can't father a bunch of kittens."

"Why Logan, that's really nice of you."

He looked around then leaned forward. "Don't you go mentioning it around the station, you hear?"

She pressed her lips together to keep from grinning. "I won't breathe a word."

"You think it's funny, but you know how guys are. I don't need to be ragged on about having a cat."

"No one's going to give you a hard time because you have a cat. Most people here are animal lovers." She thought about it. "Well, Gordon isn't a fan of cats, but my aunt has one."

He returned his attention to the file he'd been studying. She printed out a copy of the report they'd given the chief the night before and put one on Logan's desk. He looked up. "Did you say something?"

She shook her head. "Just gave you a copy of the report in case you needed it for the meeting."

"Sorry, I guess I was concentrating too hard. Thanks." He smiled briefly.

"We had the same amount of sleep last night. How is it you can look like you do?"

He grinned. "Clean living."

"Yeah, right." She sighed. "I feel like something the cat dragged in." She picked up her cup and found it empty. "Coffee. I need more coffee."

"You don't look like the cat dragged you in. You look—" he stopped.

"What?"

He reddened. "You look great."

"Wow. A compliment."

"Give me a break." He locked the file he'd been studying in his desk and stood. "Guy has to watch what he says. Don't want to be accused of sexual harassment in the workplace."

"Maybe you could give Smithers a little 411 on that matter."

"Ah, so that's his problem."

She tossed her paper cup in the trash. "One of them."

"Tess! Morning!"

She looked up. "Gordon."

He nodded at Logan. "So how's it going?"

"Good."

"Tess here showing you the ropes?"

"He knows the ropes. I'm just introducing him to the city."

"Got a big case pretty quick," he said, leaning back against the doorway to study her. "How are you feeling about that?"

Tess leaned back in her chair. "I'd like for it not to have happened. But I'm looking forward to catching this guy."

"Think you're smart enough, huh?"

"I trained with the best."

"True." He flashed a grin at Logan. "Smart girl recognizes someone of superior intelligence."

"Well, I don't know if I'd say that," she teased.

His grin vanished, and he shot her an irritated look. "Hey, I'm in Mensa."

"I was just teasing."

"Well, watch it." He glanced back as members of the force walked toward the squad room and waved at someone. "Well, we should be heading into the briefing."

"Right behind you. By the way, how is Aunt Kathy?"

But he was already out the door.

She stood and looked at Logan. He was watching her with an expression she couldn't read.

"I wish you'd say what you're thinking. Even if it's not something I want to hear."

"Hmm?" He seemed to bring himself back from somewhere. "Oh, I was just thinking that it's harder to catch serial killers because most of them are smarter than the average person."

"That can work against them as much as for them," she told him as she rounded the desk. "They like to think they're smarter than everyone—including the cops. That arrogance is what can bring them down."

"True. But we can't wait for him to trip himself up and risk him killing again."

"Agreed."

She wanted to say it was not a good idea to assume it was a male, either. But she was sure he knew that. Even if he'd been living up north, it was no secret that Florida had a female serial killer on Death Row.

She gathered the special file she'd compiled and shown to Logan the night before, the report on Toni Miller's case, and a notepad. "Ready?"

He was looking in the direction her uncle had taken. "Yeah." Picking up his own notepad, he looked around for a pen and reached over to take one from a mug filled with them on her desk.

"Hey, you're a pen thief?"

"I prefer to think of it as taking it into protective custody."

"You're just a barrel of laughs."

"Yeah, so I've heard." He gestured at the door. "After you."

Logan closed the last of the stack of files and rubbed his eyes.

"Enough reading for you?"

"Glamorous part of the job. They never show it on TV or in the movies, do they?"

Tess took the files from him and returned them to the file cabinet. "It sure wouldn't help recruitment, would it?"

He glanced at his watch. "Break for lunch?"

"Yes, please."

They walked outside and found that it had been raining and the temperature had dropped quite a bit. He rolled his shoulders to relieve the ache from sitting hunched over the files for hours.

"What do you feel like eating?"

"Food."

"I know, but what?"

"I'm too hungry to be picky," she told him. "It would be nice to eat outside or take a quick walk, though. Get some fresh air. Let's take a walk over to St. George Street."

Even though it had cooled off a little, it wasn't exactly breezy. But he figured you didn't get used to the heat by hiding from it. And if she was up for it, he was going to be.

They passed by Flagler College, housed in an old Spanish-style hotel, on the way to the Street.

"Why did you go to the University of Florida when this was closer?"

"Sam and I always wanted to go away to college, share a dorm room," she told him, her long legs matching him stride for stride. "Going to college in town just didn't seem like . . . college, you know? Besides, I really liked the criminal justice program at UF."

"What about Sam? What was her major?"

"Elementary ed. She would have made a wonderful teacher. Loved little kids, and she was good with them."

He kicked a stone out of his path. "Makes you wonder sometimes, doesn't it? The why of it all?"

She slowed her steps. "Yeah. I was angry at God for Sam's death. How could he take someone good like that and leave some of the evil people like the murderer still walking the earth and hurting even more innocent people?"

"And have you worked through that yet?"

"Hardly. At least I started attending church again. Sam and I had always loved it, and I know she wouldn't have wanted me to stop."

Her steps slowed at an elegant little restaurant, and he saw her expression turn wistful as she glanced at the menu posted on the wall of the building.

"Do you want to eat here?"

She bit her lip and then shook her head. "No, it's expensive. Besides, it's not open for lunch."

"So we'll come back at dinnertime. My treat."

"Why would you do that?" she asked, turning to face him.

He shrugged and tried to look casual. "You've shown me around, made me feel welcome in a new city."

"It's not a date."

"No, it's not a date." He found himself regretting he had to promise her. Under other circumstances, he'd like to date her, but they worked together. . . .

She stared at him for a long moment, pinning him with those sharp green eyes of hers. Then, apparently reassured, she nodded. "I'd like that even though it's taking shameless advantage of you. I think the heat's getting to you to offer to treat me at those prices. You may be eating ramen noodles for a month after the bill here."

He steeled himself not to double-check as she began walking up the street.

"Tell you what, I'll treat you to lunch," she said. "This place has good sandwiches and smoothies."

"Fine with me." Logan nearly wept when they walked into the air conditioning, but he wasn't going to say anything to Tess and look weak.

They placed their order and found seats near the window overlooking the street.

"Guess this is a big change working in a tourist town." Tess sipped her drink and handed him a couple of paper napkins.

When she glanced out the window, he used the napkins to surreptitiously wipe the perspiration from his face. He sucked the medium-size drink dry and went to refill it. When he returned, their sandwiches had arrived.

"You didn't have to wait for me," he told Tess.

She turned from looking out the window. "Well, I didn't," she said. "I was enjoying watching the rain."

He leaned forward to look out the window. The clouds had moved over, shutting out the glare of the sun. The rain slid in silvery sheets down the window, softening the day.

"I love it when it rains on the old street," Tess said.

"You love this city, period." Logan took a big bite of his turkey wrap. No question Tess knew the best places to eat.

The door opened, and a man strolled in shaking raindrops as he chose a nearby table and dropped a dusty knapsack in a chair before he went to order.

"Oh, my, they shouldn't allow the homeless to come in here," a woman said loudly near them.

Logan watched Tess glance at her, then turn back to her sandwich. The woman continued to complain, not stopping even after the man sat down with his order.

"I've had enough," Logan said quietly.

Tess nodded. "Let me handle it. I know him."

She stood and as she turned, he saw she pulled out a business card and set it on the table by the woman's plate. She picked up her drink with her other hand and strolled over to the man's table. He couldn't hear their conversation but from the man's quick, friendly smile saw that their past encounters must have been amenable.

When she returned to the table after refilling her cup at the drink station, he saw the complaining woman appeared mollified and was eating her lunch.

Tess checked her watch. "There's time for dessert, but you'll really wish later you'd saved room for the ones at Collage."

"You've steered me right in the food department so far," he said as he stood and began clearing the table.

"I'll take care of that," the waitress told. "I saw what you did, Tess," she said quietly. "Thanks."

"It was nothing."

"It wasn't nothing," Logan told her when they were outside.

She shrugged. "The woman didn't need to fear Joe. Wonder what she'd think if she knew he used to be a professor who got laid off and lost everything? We have a problem here like a lot of cities—maybe more so because it's warmer in the winter here. But we've only had a few incidents where someone got a little too aggressive panhandling."

He glanced up at the dripping skies. "Ready to take a run for it?"

They dodged the raindrops and then, a half-block later, she waved to a tourist tram turning down a side street. The tram driver stopped with a smile, and they boarded it.

Logan reached for his wallet, but the driver shook her head as she pressed the gas pedal. "No charge for the city's finest."

She let them off at the station with a wave of her hand.

Logan hated to break the mood, but he couldn't help it. "Tess, I want to take a tour of the crime scenes."

She nodded. "We should start at the lighthouse."

That was where they discovered her friend's body.

"I can go by myself."

She shook her head and turned to walk to the car in the parking lot. He noted that she kept her face averted as she fastened her seat belt. When she lifted her chin and looked out the windshield, he frowned at how pale she'd gone.

"Tess—"

"Look, you don't have to coddle me," she said, still not looking at him. "I've lived with this for years. I told you, I'm willing to do whatever it takes to catch the man who killed my friend."

He started the car and drove to the park near the lighthouse. She directed him to a parking spot and got out. He followed her as she walked, seemingly lost in thought, under huge old trees with gnarled trunks and twisted branches, dripping with Spanish moss.

"You never see trees like this up north," he told her.

She glanced up at the lighthouse, painted bright white with a thick black stripe that wound around it, then smiled at some kids who ran past, laughing.

"Sam and I pulled some of the moss down once and played with it when we were kids," she said. "We pretended it was mermaid hair. What a mess. Little bugs live in the stuff and burrow into your skin. I thought we'd go crazy until our moms got rid of them."

She walked over to a spot under one of the trees, stopped, and looked up at him. "This is where they found Sam."

Logan nodded and walked over to where she stood. He squatted down and studied the scene. Even though it had been years, he used a pen he pulled from his shirt pocket to stir the grass and look for clues for a few minutes.

When he rose, he saw that she still stood in the same place but was looking at the lighthouse. A breeze stirred the branches of the trees and raindrops fell, sprinkling her hair and catching in her eyelashes. They glittered like tears, but Tess's cheeks were dry.

"Why this place?" he asked her quietly. "Do you think there was some special reason why she was found here?"

"It's a popular place for teens to hang out at night," she said. "But I think it was because it was a favorite place for her. She worked at the lighthouse part-time. It may be she felt safe there that night when she came here with her boyfriend after the prom—although he denied leaving her there."

He moved closer and touched her cheek. "You okay?"

She nodded, and her eyes searched his.

"Looks like you have diamonds caught in your eyelashes."

"Diamonds," she whispered and looked so strange, he grabbed her arm and shook it until she shook her head and stared at him. "What?"

"What about diamonds, Tess?"

"I don't know." She backed away from him, and he let go of her arm. "I don't know."

7

Tess prowled the aisles of her aunt's quilt shop, not certain what she was looking for. She told herself she'd know it when she found it.

When she felt the prickle at the back of her neck, she turned, knowing the person she'd see.

"Gordon, haven't seen you here in ages," she said.

"Taking Kathy to lunch." He looked around. "Where is she?"

"She's just finishing up teaching a class." Tess walked to a bookcase, pulled out a book, and added it to the stack in the crook of her arm.

Gordon checked his watch. "Do me a favor and let her know I'm here? Otherwise she'll stand around talking and I want to get going."

"Sure."

Impatient as always, she couldn't help thinking as she carried the books to a planning table and stuck her head into the classroom. When her aunt looked in her direction, Tess tapped a finger on her watch. Her aunt glanced up at the clock, nodded, and dismissed the class.

The students began gathering their quilts and supplies into their tote bags and carryalls and filed out of the room. Tess caught her aunt's eye again and when she did, she tapped her finger on the third finger of her left hand. Her aunt's hand flew to her mouth, and she turned to her student who was chatting with her.

"I'm so sorry! I forgot Gordon was coming by. Would you mind having Tess help you with those directions?"

The woman shook her head and handed them to Tess. "Not at all. How've you been? Missed seeing you in the Wednesday evening class. Guess you must have been busy with the murder."

Tess nodded as she studied the directions.

"You got to catch this guy," she went on. "Why, we were talking about it at my breakfast club this morning. Gladys sleeps with a gun under her pillow."

Alarmed, Tess forgot all about the directions. "Gladys Petersen?"

"Why, yes."

Tess had pulled her over several months ago when she ran a stop sign. Gladys had claimed she didn't see the sign and from the way she was squinting, Tess had sent her for a vision test at the driver's license office. Her blood ran cold at the thought of Gladys shooting someone she couldn't see.

"Maybe I should go over and talk to her."

Then she thought about it. She'd look up the number and call first.

"Lynn, we can't guarantee anything, but so far the man has gone after—" She hesitated, then plunged on, "His victims have been younger women."

"But you don't know he won't decide to start going after women of my age."

"Serial killers tend to focus on younger women." Tess tried for a reassuring tone. "I'll be happy to talk to your breakfast club next week if you think it'll help. The best thing everyone can do is stay calm and just take the usual precautions—make sure they lock their doors and windows. Too often people make it easy for the bad guys by failing to do simple things like that."

"I'll ask the ladies if they'd like you to speak to them."

"Fine."

They put their heads together over the directions, and Tess did what she could to explain them to Lynn. Tess returned to the table where she'd left the quilt books and spread them out.

"Planning your next quilt?" Claudia asked.

She nodded and pointed to a photo of a quilt with a nautical theme. "I think I want to make one with a lighthouse in the center and scenes from the area around the border."

"Sounds lovely. Have you picked any fabrics yet?"

Tess shook her head. "Want to help?"

Claudia grinned. "Just try to stop me from making suggestions."

They roamed the several rooms filled with fabric, pulling out bolts, discussing and accepting and rejecting, until Tess's arms were piled high with bolts she carried to the cutting table.

Aunt Kathy returned from lunch and looked over the fabrics as Tess sat at the planning table. "Nice choices. Any particular reason for choosing a lighthouse?"

"Not just any lighthouse," Claudia pointed out. "Our lighthouse."

A customer walked into the shop, and she went to greet her.

Tess shrugged. "I don't know. I just want to do it."

"It's not going to be easy working on this case," Kathy said quietly. She perched on a stool next to Tess, watching her as she cut the lengths she needed for the quilt.

"No. But years ago Gordon made sure I understood what I was getting into."

When she looked up from the fabrics, she saw that her aunt's eyes were worried. "What's wrong?"

She took a deep breath, then let it out. "The job changes you, that's all."

Tess laid a hand over her aunt's. "What's wrong?"

"I just don't want you to become cynical about people. Not care as much as you do about them now."

"Is that what Gordon's done? Become cynical?" She knew the answer to that—nearly every police officer she'd worked with carried a healthy dose of cynicism about his fellow man.

"More than I knew."

"Ring me up?" Tess asked, holding out the fabrics and supplies she'd chosen along with her credit card.

"Sure."

Tess's cell rang. She pulled it from her pocket and checked the display. It was Logan. "Excuse me, I have to take this."

"Hey, Tess, are we still on tonight?"

"Yes."

"I'll pick you up at six."

"I can meet you. It's not a date, remember?"

"Right. But one thing I've learned is that parking is scarce in that area."

He was right. "Okay, pick me up. Let me give you my address."

"Really, Tess," he said with a chuckle. "See you later." He hung up.

She tucked the phone back into her pocket and saw that her aunt was smiling at her. "What?"

"Not a date, huh?"

"It isn't. He's—" She stopped when her aunt perked up. "It isn't a date."

"Who are you trying to convince?" Kathy asked.

Tess rolled her eyes. "You know, it's really not a crime to be single."

Kathy patted her cheek. "I just want you to be happy."

"I'm happy."

"You deserve a nice husband."

Tess folded her fabrics and put them in her tote bag. "I don't think it's a matter of deserving. I just think I haven't met the right man yet."

"How can you? All you do is work and fix up that house of yours."

A customer walked in. Kathy looked over, acknowledged the woman, and sent Tess a look that promised the conversation wasn't over. Tess sent up a silent thank you to the big guy upstairs and quickly threw the supplies she'd bought into the tote. She waved at her aunt, pointing at her watch to show she had to be somewhere and escaped.

"I'm a grown woman and here I am running away like a little girl," she muttered as she got into her car. Shaking her head, she checked for traffic and pulled out of the lot.

As she drove home, she found herself mentally going through the contents of her closet. She forced herself to stop. It wasn't a date, so why was she even thinking about what she was going to wear?

Logan buttoned up his shirt and debated adding a tie.

He hadn't ever lived anywhere quite so casual. Shorts and flip-flops were the uniform of the day. At night, you wore your better shorts and flip-flops. But surely a dinner at a fancy little restaurant called for a dress shirt, tie, and dark slacks. Maybe even a sport coat? He pulled one off a hanger and laid it over his arm.

Joe lay in the middle of the bed washing himself.

"Big date, huh? Oh, maybe it's not a date."

Logan took a final look in the mirror and left the room. Maybe he should have asked Tess how dressy he had to be for the restaurant . . .

Then he chided himself. Tess didn't strike him as the type to be overly concerned with such things. He walked into the kitchen to make sure Joe had food and water. The cat followed him, looked in the dish, and turned his nose up at it.

"Maybe I'll bring you home a doggie bag," Logan told him. "Cat bag? Leftovers. If there are any."

Grabbing his car keys, he left the house, laying his jacket carefully on the back seat. The minute he started the car he turned on the air conditioner. The temperature had dropped some and there was a little bit of a breeze, but he wanted to make sure she was cool riding to the restaurant.

When he pulled into her driveway, Logan tried not to stare as she came out of her house. She wore a spaghetti-strapped black dress showing off her curves and her golden tan. Her only jewelry was a long rope of some sparkly stones. Strappy, black high-heeled sandals made her legs seem even longer than usual. Her hair was always tucked into a fancy little bun thing at the nape of her neck but tonight she wore it loose and flowing over her shoulders.

Wow. Double-wow. The everyday Tess was pretty. This nighttime Tess looked stunning.

"Hi," she said, sliding into the passenger seat.

"You look nice." Lame, he thought. But better to err on the side of caution with a partner.

Tess tugged at the hem of her skirt. "Thanks. I can't remember the last time I got dressed up." She glanced at him. "You look nice, too."

"I brought a sport coat. I wasn't sure if I needed one."

"We're pretty casual in Florida. It's totally up to you."

"You're not cold, are you?"

"I'm fine."

He tried to ignore the faint scent of her perfume—something light and lemony—drifting toward him. "I'm hungry. I hope this isn't one of those places where they act all arrogant and give you little bitty portions?"

She laughed. "No, Aunt Kathy and Gordon went there for their anniversary, and they were both very pleased with their dinners."

He parked, and they got out and walked the short distance to the restaurant.

"Tell you what, if you're still hungry after we eat, I'll treat you to a pizza on the way home."

He grinned. "Sounds fair. Joe'll like that, too."

"Joe?"

"The cat."

"'The cat,' not 'my cat'?"

"The goal's to find him a home."

"So he likes pizza, huh?"

"Yeah. Pepperoni."

Logan opened the door and delicious scents poured out as Tess walked inside. The lighting was low, the mood intimate. They were seated at a small table in a secluded corner, and a server came immediately.

"Good evening, folks," he said. "Are we celebrating any special occasion tonight?"

Logan looked at Tess.

She smiled. "Just a nice dinner. Logan's new in town."

"Well, welcome to St. Augustine," the man said.

They ordered sweet tea and spent a few minutes studying the menu.

"I warned you about the prices," she whispered.

He made a dismissive motion with his hand. "It's good to get out someplace nice like this once in a while, don't you think?"

Tess settled back against her upholstered chair. "It *is* nice. I always wondered what it would be like to eat here. Dine," she corrected herself. "We eat at some restaurants. We *dine* at places like this one."

She spread her napkin on her lap and smiled at him. "I hoped we'd come here for dinner before the prom but of course it was way beyond the budget of a high school boy." She sighed. "Everything looks good. What are you going to order?"

"The steak. I know, predictable, but I saw one go past on the server's tray and it looked good. You?"

"The lobster ravioli. The ravioli's not just stuffed with lobster, it comes with a lobster tail."

"So, can friends share the 'baked Brie for two'?"

She made a face at him. "Very funny."

They chatted easily over the appetizer—kind of a fancy way to serve cheese, in Logan's opinion but it seemed like a night to try new things. Well, the steak wasn't new, but the way the menu described it, he figured it was new for him. The cheese came wrapped in flaky pastry with apple chutney on top. He'd never tried chutney, but it tasted so good that Tess was going to have to eat fast or he'd be taking more than his share.

The diners seated at nearby tables were mostly couples although there was a small group here and there. Logan liked looking over occasionally at one elderly couple who sat holding hands while they enjoyed their meal.

Tess saw them, too. "Anniversary? Wonder how long they've been together?"

"Who knows. They remind me of my parents. The two of them always looked happy together."

"I'm sorry. It's tough to lose family."

"And friends who become family, like Sam."

She nodded. "Like Sam."

A waiter carried a small cake to the table, and the couple beamed.

Tess and Logan exchanged a look. "Has to be an anniversary. Or a birthday."

They finished dinner and asked to see the dessert menu.

"I could read this menu all night," Tess said. "Listen to this: 'to celebrate our beautiful bougainvillea tree, we have created a special dessert of strawberries sautéed in butter and black pepper, vanilla bean ice cream, and Cabernet vanilla sauce in a crispy phyllo cup.'"

"A strawberry sundae," he told her.

"Sure. Just like what we ate was just ravioli, and steak, and cheese in pastry. I'm getting it. What are you having?"

"Rum cake."

She scanned the description. "Sounds good, too."

Tess excused herself, and Logan called the waiter over.

When she returned, the couple was leaving the restaurant. Both of them looked puzzled, but happy.

Logan's cell vibrated. He pulled it out and checked the display. "Sorry, Tess, I have to take this. It's about a case back home. Be right back."

"There's a quiet place back near the restrooms."

"Great. Go ahead and eat your dessert. This'll just take a moment."

When he returned, Tess was setting her spoon down on her plate with a sigh.

He grinned as he sat down. "That good?"

"I managed to save you some," she told him. "It's only because I'm so glad we came here tonight. Otherwise, there's no way I could be so generous."

Logan looked at the dish she pushed toward him. Barely a tablespoon of the strawberry sauce sat atop a small dollop of ice cream. But he was enjoying the way she looked so relaxed and happy, and he played along with her supposed generous gesture.

He spooned it up and tasted strawberry heaven—rich berries that were sweet, but with the dash of butter and black pepper it had a unique flavor like nothing he'd tasted before.

"I'm getting this next time we come." He took a bite of his cake and pushed the plate toward her so that she could taste it.

"We're coming again?"

He met her look. "I hope so."

She nodded slowly. "I'd like that."

The waiter came to ask if they wanted more coffee, and when they declined, he left their bill.

"That was a sweet thing you did."

Logan looked up from putting his credit card in the leather envelope with the bill. "What? Offer you a bite of my cake?"

"I know you paid the check for that couple."

"Don't know what you're talking about."

"Sure you do."

Logan pinned the man with a look as he picked up the bill.

"You didn't say I couldn't tell her," he said. "You just said I couldn't tell the couple."

"Let me have the bill back," Logan said easily. "I think I'll cross off that tip . . . "

"Yes sir." The man gulped, but handed it over.

Logan pushed the bill back into the man's hands. "Just kidding."

When they walked outside, a soft breeze carried the scent of the ocean nearby and rustled the branches of the bougainvillea tree. Delicate fuchsia-colored petals drifted down to dance on the cobbled street. People walked up and down the street, enjoying their evening. A man strummed a guitar and sang about pirates of old as he sat on the sidewalk, his guitar case open to receive tips.

"I'm falling in love with this city of yours," Logan told her. "Gordon told me I would."

"Gordon? He told you you'd like the city? When did he say that?"

"When I came here for the interview. He was right about you, too."

She stopped and stared at him. "What?"

"He said the department had a crackerjack detective I'd want to work with."

8

Crackerjack. He used the term 'crackerjack'?"

"Yeah. You've never heard him describe you that way?"

Tess shook her head. She began walking toward the car again. Logan walked beside her, his hands in his pockets.

"You knew he wrote me?"

"No."

Logan nodded. "Right after my team solved the Blanco serial killer case. Said he was on the recruitment committee and the department was looking for a new detective. He invited me to come down and talk to the committee about the job, take a look around the city, and see if it was a place I might like to live."

He glanced at her. "He never told you about this?"

"No. Not that he talks much about upper level stuff to me. And we downplay the fact that he's married to my aunt when we're at the station. I don't need anyone to think I got my job because of nepotism."

He paused at the car. "It's a little early to head home, and it's such a nice night. Want to take a walk?"

"Not in these shoes."

"Oh. Hadn't thought about that."

"Yeah. Men don't. They just like—" She stopped.

"They just like what?"

She refused to say more. He knew men liked seeing women wear high heels. She didn't need to tell him so—it would imply she'd worn them for him and she hadn't. She'd worn them because she liked them, although right about now she wished she'd worn something more comfortable. . . .

"Tell you what. Why don't we go for a carriage ride? I've never been on one."

It was a beautiful night—the air had that soft quality to it when the temperature and ever-present Florida humidity had dropped as summer began fading. And dinner out with Logan had been so enjoyable. Surely, she could humor him by taking such a ride.

They drove around to the seawall near the Old Fort where the carriages waited for passengers.

A driver welcomed them with a tip of his hat and said he was available to take them for a ride.

Tess was about to climb up the step to the carriage when Logan held out a hand. "Will you let me help you?"

She hesitated and then nodded. Aunt Kathy would say he possessed manners and accepting help wasn't a sign of weakness. If he were wearing something as impractical as heeled sandals, she'd help him. A giggle escaped her lips at the thought.

Logan climbed aboard and sat beside her on the leather seat. "What's so funny?"

So she told him.

His eyebrows went up, and his mouth quirked in a grin. "I'd say you had a little too much to drink, but we both had sweet tea." He leaned back in the seat and regarded her. "I'm glad we did this tonight. I think we've both needed a break from work."

"Nice night for a ride," their driver said as he flicked the reins and got his horse going. "Look at that moon!"

They looked. It rose slowly over the fort, casting the structure in a mysterious mix of light and shadow.

"Where are you folks from?"

"Here."

He turned and shot them a grin. "Well, how about that. So you two want the quiet tour or the regular one? I don't charge mo' money for the talking one," he said with a chuckle.

"My friend here is new to the town," Tess told him, shooting Logan a grin. "Why don't you give him the talking one so he knows about this place he's landed?"

So the driver gave them the tour as the horse pulled the carriage, and it felt like it always did when she took a ride on one—like a trip back in time with the clip-clop of horse hooves on cobblestone and on paved roads. The carriage bore old-fashioned lamps that cast a gentle glow and a blanket to pull over your lap if the night grew cool.

The beam from the lighthouse cut through some low-lying clouds, sending a signal to any mariners out this night. Tess thought the sight of it was reassuring and yet a little remote and sad. She turned slightly to watch it as the carriage moved along the waterfront.

"You okay?"

When she glanced back at him, the breeze sent a long strand of her hair across her face. He caught it and tucked it behind her ear in a gesture unexpected and intimate. Her eyes widened, and her throat went dry.

"Sorry," he said, jerking his hand back.

"It's okay," she said and her cheeks warmed as she heard the huskiness in her voice.

She wasn't surprised at her reaction to his touch. The carriage ride on a beautiful summer night with the moon rising and a soft breeze coming off the water after a relaxing and delicious dinner. A handsome man she'd found such an intelligent and compatible partner at work, who also seemed attracted to her.

Dangerous combination.

"You looked sad."

She shrugged. "I know buildings don't have emotions, but the lighthouse always looks like a little lonely to me."

"It had to be a lonely life for the man who tended it," he said thoughtfully. "Some of them didn't have families and even if they did, they could be the only ones for miles and miles."

The horse pranced in place, eager to make the turn at the light. Tess remembered how the carriage horses stepped lively through the intersection from her days at her part-time job.

And then another memory struck her as she gazed at the two big marble lions guarding its base. Suddenly Tess could hear Sam crying. She tensed as the memory washed over her like a relentless tide, as real and vivid as the night she'd wept on Tess's shoulder. Sam's boyfriend had driven over the bridge in his beloved sports car and pretended to hear the lions baying at her. Local legend had it that they roared whenever a chaste young woman crossed the bridge, and he jeered at her because she wanted to save herself for marriage.

"What is it? What are you remembering?"

She turned to him. "Sam came to me crying about her boyfriend the day before she was killed," she said. "He didn't want to take no for an answer."

"He was discounted as a suspect fairly early on, wasn't he?"

Tess frowned. "Some of us thought too early. His parents are wealthy and prominent in the community."

"So maybe we need to take another look at him?"

"I'd like to," she said, watching him for his reaction. "I remember no one took me seriously when I tried to tell them what she said."

"You're not a teenage girl without influence this time. You're a woman with the ability to speak for your friend."

She nodded and smiled slightly. "So hear me roar? Let's go talk to Wendell Hendricks, Jr., tomorrow."

Logan dug through the files and did some research before Tess got to the office the next day.

He wanted to know more about Sam's boyfriend. While it might seem like an advantage to grow up in the area and know many people, it could be a positive to not know them and look on things in an entirely new way.

Wendell Hendricks, Jr., had followed in his father's foot-steps and now worked as an attorney in his firm. His wife of five years, Muffi Langston Hendricks, was also an associate at the firm. The local newspaper featured photographs of them attending numerous events in local society.

Tess rushed in. "Sorry. Court case ran late."

"No problem. I've been doing some light reading on Hendricks."

He watched the way she moved to sit behind her computer and wondered if there'd be any awkwardness after last night . . . would she think he'd overstepped when he touched her hair? She logged onto her computer and seemed all business. He looked down at the file and when he glanced up a few min-utes later, he caught her looking at him.

"About—"

She shook her head. "Not here."

They were alone in the office but he nodded.

"Just give me a minute so I can check for messages, then we'll go. I told Hendricks we'd be there about noon."

A few minutes later, she stood and grabbed her notepad. "Ready?"

"Sure."

He waited until they were in the car and out of the parking lot before he turned to her. "Afraid the office is bugged?"

"If I say yes, will you think I'm paranoid?"

"Yes, but it could be true. I've heard of stations that did it. Best to err on the side of caution if you're not comfortable with being overheard. I just wanted to say that I had a great time last night."

She glanced at him briefly and smiled. "I did, too."

"So we're okay?"

"Why wouldn't we be?"

He wasn't a dummy. "No reason."

"You're a strange man, Logan."

They drove to the law firm and parked. Logan glanced up at the elaborately redone Victorian building and whistled. "Wow. Some digs."

Tess didn't say anything as they walked into the building.

Hendricks stood when his assistant ushered them into his office. "Why, Tess, what a surprise."

"We called ahead."

"I know. I haven't seen you in years." He stepped around a massive desk and shook Logan's hand. "Wendell Hendricks."

"Logan McMillan."

"Have a seat. Can I get you some coffee? Perrier?"

"We're fine. Detective Villanova and I are investigating Samantha Marshall's murder."

"That was years ago."

"No statute of limitations on murder."

"No, no, I'm sure not and there shouldn't be," he said quickly. "I just thought you'd be working on the latest murder."

"We are," Tess spoke up.

"So they're connected."

"We're looking at all the angles," Logan said. "I'd like to ask you some questions about Ms. Marshall."

"I answered them all at the time."

Logan knew from what he'd read in the file and what Tess had said about Hendricks's father stepping in and shutting down questioning pretty quickly after the murder.

"Never hurts to go over things again, see if anything was missed."

Wendell sat back in his leather chair, steepled his fingers, and looked at Logan over them. "True. It's just hard to remember much. It's been years."

"Not that many," Tess responded briefly.

"I'm sorry, I know this must be painful for you," Wendell said. "The two of you were friends."

Tess flipped open her notepad. "How long did you and Sam date?"

"You'd know the answer to that—"

"Forget that we know each other, Wendell, and just answer the question."

Wendell looked irritated, but quickly masked his expression. "We dated for a few months our senior year."

"And you were together at the prom?"

"Yes, I was her date."

"Were you and Sam having any problems before that night?"

"No."

"But she left the prom that night after what we understand was a disagreement?"

Wendell spread his hands. "A minor misunderstanding. I danced one dance with another girl. It was petty high school drama."

Logan watched Tess's reaction. She and Sam had been close friends. But if Wendell had hoped Tess would react to his remark with emotion, he was wrong.

"How so, Wendell?" she asked calmly.

"There was no need to go off in a jealous snit."

"And you feel Sam did this?"

He shrugged. "I think the facts speak for themselves."

"And where were you during the time she left the prom?"

"At the prom, of course."

"According to statements by two witnesses, there was a forty-five minute period when no one saw you."

"I left for a few minutes to look for Sam. But it was just for a few minutes."

Logan tapped his pen on his notepad and studied Wendell. He didn't have a high opinion of attorneys in general, but there was something about this guy that just bothered him.

"Maybe it's time for you to meet someone," Wendell said. He picked up his phone and punched in a number. "Can you come in here for a moment? Thanks."

The door to the office opened and a woman walked in. She wore a lot of gold jewelry and a white suit that clung to her curves.

Tess lifted her brows. "Muffi."

The woman inclined her blond head. "Tess." She glanced at Logan. "And who's this? I don't believe we've met." She offered her hand.

Logan rose and introduced himself.

"Muffi, the detectives are here asking questions about Samantha. You remember, from high school."

"Yes, terrible tragedy. So, Tess, you're a detective already? I guess these things go quickly when you have relatives in the business."

"No, they don't. I had to take a test."

Muffi's eyes narrowed. She turned to Wendell. "Darling, why did you call me in here?"

Wendell looked at Tess, then Logan. "I would appreciate it if you keep what Muffi is about to tell you confidential."

Logan exchanged a glance with Tess. "All right."

"Muffi, Tess and Logan say there was about forty-five minutes where I was away from the prom."

She nodded. "Well, this is rather embarrassing. You have to remember Wendell and I were just teenagers at our senior prom."

"Go on," Tess said.

Muffi shrugged. "Well, I know where Wendell was. He was with me, making out in his car in the parking lot."

9

So that was a surprise, huh?"

Tess fastened her seat belt and slid on her sunglasses. "A little convenient, don't you think?"

"A good attorney always has an ace up his sleeve. Actually, that's a bad example."

"It doesn't prove anything," she said, drumming her fingertips on her knee. "She could be lying for him. He could be lying for her."

Logan braked for a stoplight. "They could be lying for each other."

Her head jerked around, and she stared at him. "You don't think . . . "

"There have been killers who worked in tandem. It's unlikely, but not outside the realm of possibility."

"They'd have started young," she mused.

"Killers have started much younger. We'll add the lawyer and his trophy wife to our list of possible suspects."

"A list of one," she said. Propping her elbow on the window, she stared out the window.

"Every list starts with one."

She turned to him. "You're being awfully optimistic."

"The whole business can wear you down," he told her. "These cases aren't solved quickly. Sometimes we don't solve them. It's important to keep some perspective if you can."

She sighed. "Yeah. I know you're right."

"What do you want to do for lunch?"

"I don't care. You pick."

"How about we pick up some subs and take them someplace to eat?"

"You mean like a picnic?"

"Yeah."

She pushed her sunglasses up on top of her head. "It hasn't cooled off enough to do that yet."

"Who's the wimp now?"

"I'm not picking you up and carrying you to the car when you pass out from sunstroke." She waved her hand at a bank sign. "Look at the temp."

"Okay. Maybe not yet. Is it going to be cool soon?"

"October."

"October? Wow."

"It's Florida."

"Yeah, I know. I just never expected it to be so warm so long."

"Sorry to tell you it won't snow for Christmas."

He chuckled. "You just crack me up, you know that?"

"Yeah, I know, Yankee." She frowned when he pulled into a restaurant parking lot. "This place? Again?"

"You said for me to pick."

She got out and pretended to grumble. It was one of her favorite places to eat, but she wasn't going to tell him that. The place had good food, and it overlooked the water. Today, sailboats were chasing a brisk wind.

They ordered their food and then sat staring at the view.

"Do you like to sail?"

Tess pulled her gaze from the sailboats. "Never been."

"You've lived around this gorgeous water and never been on a sailboat?"

She shook her head and smiled at the waitress when she brought her sandwich. "You?"

"I used to sail a lot in Chicago. Maybe we can go sometime."

"I'd like that."

She wanted to go over the case with him, but they had to be careful not to do it where they could be overheard. Pretty sad, she told herself, when all you wanted to do with a handsome man was talk about work.

"So if there's no snow, how can it feel like Christmas?" he asked her, picking up a French fry, dipping it into a puddle of ketchup on his plate, and popping it into his mouth.

"I've never even seen snow," she told him.

He gaped at her. "Never?"

She shook her head. "It's not so odd. Some people never do. Besides, what's so great about snow?"

He glanced out the window. "It's cold. That alone should recommend it about now."

"Okay. What else?"

"It's pretty and white."

"Until it melts and becomes all dirty and slushy."

He offered her a French fry. "I don't believe you have no romance in you, Tess."

She took it. "What can I say?"

"I saw the way you enjoyed the restaurant that night," he told her. "I think you're very romantic." He reached across the table and touched her hand.

The sounds of the restaurant faded, and the world narrowed down to just the two of them. Tess felt a flutter of nerves.

"Logan—"

"Spoilsport," he said as he let go of her hand.

They ate in silence for a few minutes. "So you miss sailing and snow. What else?"

She watched him hesitate for a moment and reached across the table to put her hand on his. "Talk to me. I still don't know half as much about you as you do me."

He turned her hand over and squeezed it, then withdrew it so that he could pull out his wallet. She watched him take out several photos and spread them on the table before her.

Tess's eyes widened. He and another man sat on a hospital bed. Both of them were bald. It felt like her heart leaped into her throat.

"I miss my buddy, Jason, most of all. He died last year. Cancer."

"You shaved your head when he was doing chemo, didn't you?"

He shrugged. "A bunch of us on the force did. It was the least we could do."

"I'm sorry."

Logan slid the photos back into his wallet and returned it to his back pocket. "So I know a little about how you feel about losing a friend."

She nodded. "So are you still angry?"

He pushed his plate away. "You bet. Why do people like Jason have to die and the scum live to a ripe old age?"

"I've struggled with that," she said quietly. "It's the big question, isn't it? But I think I'm coming to terms with it. My pastor's helped me a lot."

"I haven't been inside a church since Jason's memorial service. Don't know if I'll ever be able to."

"Let me know if you'd ever like to visit—"

Her cell went off. She checked the display, then took the call. When she finished, she took a last, long drink of her tea.

"We have to run by Mrs. Ramsey's. She called in, said some-one broke in. We can swing by her house and still make the meeting at the station."

"Again?" He tipped up his drink, took a last swallow. "Why do you always take the calls for her?"

She smiled at him. "I asked to take them. I owe her."

<hr />

Logan wasn't good with meetings.

Tess wasn't either.

Every time he glanced at her sitting next to him she was doodling on her note pad. When Gordon walked into the room, Logan gave Tess a nudge with his elbow and slanted his eyes at her uncle in a silent message. Tess flipped a clean page over as if she were taking notes.

"People, we need some progress," the team leader said in a resigned voice. "We've had a stalemate on this for two weeks now."

The door opened again, and Logan glanced up. Maria from Records stood there, her face pale.

"Maria. I—uh, we're discussing progress right now," the leader said, getting to his feet. "I'll come brief you as soon as we're done."

"Progress," she said in a dull voice. "Does that mean you've found Toni's killer?"

"We're doing everything we can."

Maria began sobbing. Tess got to her feet and walked over to put her arm around her. She spoke quietly so that Logan didn't hear, but Maria nodded and let Tess lead her out of the room. Someone shut the door behind them, and the meeting resumed.

When Tess returned, her cheeks were pale, and Logan could see that her eyelashes were wet. She stared straight ahead as different team members gave their reports. They'd already agreed he would give theirs, and Logan sent up a silent thank you.

Strategy was discussed for the following week, assignments for follow-ups with neighbors, and the trickle of leads that came in on a tip hotline.

The meeting broke up and people began filing out of the room.

When Logan and Tess walked outside into the bright sunlight, he tried to shake off the depression he felt. He didn't even need to look at Tess to know she was feeling the same way—he could sense it.

"We need a break."

"Duh." She got into the car and sat there staring sightlessly through the windshield.

"No, I mean a break away from all of this." He started the car. "How long will it take for you to change?"

"Change into what?"

"Change into something you can wear sailing."

She gave a short laugh as she buckled her seat belt. "Did you buy a boat while we were in the meeting?"

"They have sailboats at the marina, don't they?"

"Yeah."

"So we're going to rent one for an hour or two."

"What if I have plans?"

He glanced at her. "Do you?"

"I was going to go to my quilting guild."

"You're at the quilt shop an awful lot. Spend some time with me, Tess." He said it quietly and caught himself holding his breath.

And he wasn't real happy when she hesitated.

"I spent all day with you."

"Not the same thing. But if you don't want to—"

"I want to," she said finally.

A tourist walked into the path of the car in front of the fort. Logan slammed on the brakes, and his arm went out to keep Tess from moving forward.

"Sorry," he said when he accidentally touched her. "Reflex."

She gave him a mild look. "It's okay. Wow, guy's guardian angel was on duty today."

"I oughta give him a ticket," he muttered. "Next time he might not be so lucky and he'll get hurt."

He didn't have to worry about that. A uniformed officer sitting at one of the outdoor tables of a nearby restaurant had seen what happened. He threw down his napkin and met the jaywalker when he stepped onto the sidewalk.

Logan and Tess exchanged a look.

"Do you believe in divine justice?" she asked him suddenly.

"That was man's justice."

A horn honked. Logan waved a hand in apology at the driver behind him and resumed driving.

"I know. I just wondered if you believed that God takes care of punishing those who sin."

"I sure hope so," he said. "Because I know we'll never catch everyone who does."

He pulled into her driveway. "This going to take long?"

She made a face at him. "Five minutes."

"Yeah, sure," he said.

Tess lifted her chin. "Time me."

Logan checked his watch. "You're on. Winner buys dinner."

She fairly leaped out of the car and ran to her door. In what seemed like a moment later, she was backing out, pulling out her weapon, and gesturing at him to join her.

He got out of the car, drew his weapon, and joined her.

"Someone's been in the house."

She went in first and he backed her, then they split up and moved through each room.

"Clear!" she called.

"Clear."

Tess slid her gun back in its holster. "Okay, now you're really going to think I'm paranoid."

"Trust your gut," he told her, still tense as he looked around. "Tell me what looks off."

"Someone straightened up a little." She shook her head, puzzled. "The couch pillows are in different places, and I'd left the newspaper scattered over the top of the coffee table. Stuff like that."

"Boyfriend?"

She frowned. "You know I don't have a boyfriend."

He knew he wanted to be her boyfriend. Shaking his head as if to clear it, he walked around the room. Talk about neat.

"Remember that case on the news a month or two ago?" he asked her. "Woman broke into someone's house, cleaned it, then left a bill?"

"Yeah."

"You said your mother died. Would any friends do this?"

Tess smacked her forehead with her hand. "My aunt. She has a key. I always say she's obsessive compulsive. She must have come by."

She walked into the kitchen and opened the refrigerator. "Yup. Look what my burglar did." She pulled out a baked chicken, a Tupperware container of potato salad, and one of baked beans.

"Wow."

She opened one cupboard, then another and she grinned. "She grocery shopped for me. When I was at the shop the other day, I complained I hadn't had time with all the overtime we've worked with the murder. I know, you're thinking I went to quilting class and could have gone shopping instead."

"Hey, you needed a break. I don't care for grocery shopping myself." He eyed the food. "I don't suppose you'd consider bringing the chicken along for the sail?"

"Absolutely. Seems destined, don't you think? If you don't mind packing it all up while I change, there's a picnic basket in the garage."

"I'm on it."

The garage was as neat as the inside of the house. Logan found the basket easily and packed the chicken, potato salad, and beans, then added the jug of sweet tea he found on the shelf in the refrigerator. He'd stop by the grocery store tomorrow and replace everything, but for now it saved time and was just what he was hungry for when he hadn't known he'd been hungry for it.

Maybe his guardian angel was on duty for him today as well.

Tess returned wearing a baseball cap with the St. Augustine PD insignia, her hair in a long tail pulled through the back of it. Her T-shirt was long-sleeved but her shorts . . . well, they made it seem like her legs went on forever.

"I packed sunscreen for us. I have to warn you: I don't have any motion sickness pills, and I didn't do so well the last time I went for one of those river cruises."

He shrugged and picked up the picnic basket. "We can stop for some if you want."

"I'm sure I'll be fine. We're not going to be out that long, right?"

"Right." As much as he wanted to keep her out for hours, they didn't have all that much daylight left.

"So, this aunt of yours who straightens up and leaves food for you," Logan said as he locked the door. "You think she'd consider adopting me?"

10

Tess watched Logan guide the sailboat out of the crowded marina and then, when they were clear, he hoisted the sail and the boat sped across the sparkling water.

Bliss. She lifted her face to the sun and sighed. "This was such a great idea. Whose idea was it?"

Logan laughed. "You're not going to try to take credit for it, are you?"

"Wish I could. Perfect end to the day."

"How are you doing?"

The man saw everything. "Well, I wish I'd had some motion sickness pills on hand, but I think I'll be okay."

He tacked the sails with competent hands and the boat slowed. "Let's just take it easy for a few minutes and see how it goes. We're not in a race. We're out here to relax. And next time we'll bring those pills for you."

Next time. Sounded like a promise. She liked the sound of that.

But she didn't like the fact she couldn't control her body's reaction to the motion of the waves.

They'd stopped at his house so he could change into a white T-shirt, khakis, and deck shoes. She liked the way he looked so relaxed and at ease as he stood with his hands steady on the wheel.

"So, you think you're going to get a sailboat?"

"Will you come sailing with me, if I do?"

She nodded. She had a feeling she might be buying a lot of motion sickness pills.

"Hungry yet?"

"I was born hungry," she said with a sigh.

They dropped anchor and dug into the food. Well, Logan did. Tess took it careful, eating a little roast chicken and a few small spoonfuls of the potato salad and baked beans. Everything tasted good, but she decided to be cautious. She could always have more at home later, if she was still hungry.

The sun, the breeze, the rocking motion of the boat . . . they all combined to make Tess drowsy after her busy day. She slapped a hand over her mouth as a huge yawn overtook her. "Sorry. I don't know why I'm suddenly so sleepy."

She sighed as she leaned back on the bench and stared up at the sail fluttering in the breeze off the water. "It's so beautiful out here. No wonder why you love sailing."

"Maybe you're finally truly relaxing."

The sailboat rocked gently. They could see all the movement on the shore, but out here it was quiet and restful.

"Did you get enough to eat?"

"I'm stuffed." He patted his stomach. "Your aunt's baked chicken was amazing."

"Sorry you couldn't eat the potato salad. I didn't realize you were allergic to onions."

"Her baked beans more than made up for it."

Tess yawned again and reached for her sweet tea. Maybe the caffeine would help. She watched as her hand missed the glass, and she had to concentrate on picking it up. The plastic glass slipped from her hand and fell onto the deck. Funny thing . . . she didn't care. She watched it roll onto the deck.

"Tess? Tess? Are you okay?"

She blinked. It was hard to focus, and her head felt so heavy she felt like she had to hold it up.

Logan's face came nearer. "What's the matter with you?"

"I'm just so tired," she whispered. Talking took too much effort. She pulled her legs up and stretched out on the bench she'd been sitting on. "I'm sorry, can you take me home? I need to go to bed."

She felt his hands grasp her arms and shake her. "Tess, did you take something at the house? You said you didn't have any motion sickness pills."

"No . . . didn't have any," she muttered, feeling irritable. "Need to sleep. That's all. You sail on without me."

She batted away his hand when he touched her eye, but he was relentless, holding the lid open so that too much sun poured in, making her head hurt.

"Your pupils are dilated," he said, doing the same thing to the other one.

"Just let me sleep for a few minutes," she begged, curling up into a ball.

"Something's wrong," she heard him say, and it seemed like he was talking from a long way away.

"I'm fine," she insisted. But something didn't seem right.

"You're sure you didn't take anything?"

"No."

She heard a rustling and forced her heavy eyelids open. He was searching through her purse. "Hey, that's private property."

"Sue me," he muttered. "You don't even have an aspirin in here. Did you take something at your house?"

"You asked me that." Her head fell back against the bench. She heard snoring. Someone was snoring. Was he sleeping, too?

She heard talking. Logan was talking to someone. Who else was on the boat? Feeling groggy, she blinked. He was using his cell phone. Rude. That was rude. She shouldn't be sleeping, but he had asked her to come out here with him, and now he was talking with someone he called Zach.

It was tough to sit up but she forced herself up, forced her eyes to open. Rag doll. She felt like a rag doll, no spine at all. Then she came to attention and went rigid. Waves of nausea came over her, slow at first and then stronger. The shoreline bobbed up and down. Her stomach roiled. She leaned over the side of the boat and threw up.

"Tess!" Logan shouted, and she felt his hand grasp the back of her shirt. "Hold on, she's throwing up again!" he yelled.

The cell phone plunked onto the cushion beside her. She could hear someone shouting, but she couldn't understand what they were saying. Logan's arms went around her, and he dragged her back against him.

"No, I have to throw up again!" she cried, and he relaxed his hold but held onto her as she leaned over the side and retched until her sides hurt and collapsed against him.

"I've got to get you back to shore," he said. "Hold on, Tess. You're going to be all right."

She'd had flu so bad once she'd been hospitalized and wondered if she were going to survive. But this was the sickest she could ever be. She was no drama queen, but she thought she was going to die.

Logan hadn't felt so helpless since he sat beside his friend Jason's bed as he talked about dying.

"Hang on, Tess, I'm going to get you some help." He cradled her in one arm as he dialed 911, identified himself, and told the dispatcher he needed a paramedic. She got the information from him and promised help would be waiting at the dock.

He laid her on the bench and kept an eye on her as he pulled up the anchor, turned the boat around, and headed to shore. The trip took only minutes, but they seemed to drag like hours.

Two paramedics came onto the boat and assessed Tess. She was still pale, but it seemed like she was starting to come around.

"Hey there, pretty lady, can you tell me your name?"

"You know very well that it's Tess," she said tartly, flinching as he shone a light into her eyes. "Geez, Hank, you gotta be pretty desperate to flirt with me looking like this."

"Desperate's his middle name," the other paramedic responded with a grin as he wrapped a blood pressure cuff around her arm.

Hank snickered and turned to Logan. "So tell me her symptoms."

Logan met Tess's gaze. She wasn't just the woman he cared about—she was his partner, another law enforcement officer. He didn't know what had happened, but he did as he'd advised her earlier at her house: he trusted his gut. Tess wouldn't do drugs. Something in the food had made her sick.

Hank listened to Logan describe how Tess had become lethargic, then almost unresponsive, and how she'd thrown up until it seemed she couldn't any longer. When Logan mentioned the picnic they'd brought, Hank examined the contents of the basket and sniffed at them.

"But you didn't get sick?"

Logan shook his head. "Oh, but I didn't eat the potato salad."

Hank shook his head. "People think they can get sick on potato salad when it's warm, but that's pretty much a thing of the past when people made their own mayonnaise."

He turned to Tess. "Let's get you seen by a doc at the ER."

"Oh, such a fuss over nothing," she complained. "I'm already feeling better."

"Tess, please don't argue," Logan said quietly.

She stared at him for a long moment and then she sighed. "Oh, fine. But I'm walking to the ambulance."

"Thank goodness," Hank said. "Garrett and I weren't looking forward to carting you off the boat."

It was the perfect thing to say. Logan watched in amusement as Tess stood, looking miffed, and held out her hand to him. It was a gesture that meant more than words to him. He clasped it and they stepped from the boat together. She looked at him in surprise when he climbed into the ambulance with her after helping her inside.

"You don't have to go with me."

"Just try to stop me."

She sat down on the gurney and sighed. "I couldn't even if I wanted to." Her eyes were moist when she looked at him. "Thank you."

Logan paced while they examined Tess in the emergency room. As hard as it had been to visit Jason at the hospital, it had always been worse when there was some reason why he had to wait outside while his friend received treatment or the doctor was in consultation with him.

Finally, he pulled rank, showed a clerk his badge.

"Cubicle Three."

He strode down the hall and nearly ran into a harried-looking doctor coming out of the cubicle.

"Let me guess: Mr. McMillan?"

Logan stopped. "That's me."

"Ms. Villanova is doing fine. I think it's a bad case of motion sickness, but I'm running some tests. Fortunately for us, she threw up again while she was in the exam room. I'm going to send her home, but bring her back if there's any sign she's getting sick again."

"You're sure she shouldn't spend the night?"

The doctor looked at him over his glasses. "I've known Tess since grade school. I wouldn't dare try keeping her if she didn't want to stay. And trust me, she doesn't want to stay."

Sure enough, she was sitting up on the gurney going over discharge instructions with a nurse before the doctor could walk away.

"Is there anyone you don't know in this city?" he demanded.

She blinked. "Not many. Why?"

He shook his head. "It seems like everyone I run into knows you."

Tess stood. "That isn't always a good thing as you saw with Hank and Garrett."

A nurse walked in pushing a wheelchair. "No arguing. Hospital policy."

To his surprise, Tess accepted without an argument. The nurse, an older woman with a determined look, winked at him as she pushed the chair from the cubicle.

"That woman scares me," Tess admitted when the nurse left them at the cashier's window.

"Tess, honey, you okay?" she heard a woman call.

Tess turned. "Aunt Kathy! What are you doing here?"

"Little bird called me." Kathy smiled at Logan. She looked back at Tess. "You okay, honey? What happened?"

"It's no big deal," Tess told her. "I just got sick when we were out sailing."

Kathy stroked her hair. "You feeling better?"

"I'm fine, thanks. Can you drive us back to Logan's car at the marina?"

"Sure thing. Gordon's waiting out in the parking lot."

Gordon pulled up as they went outside. "Need a lift?" he asked with a grin.

"Thanks," Tess told him as she stepped from the wheelchair and got into the back seat.

"You're welcome," Gordon said, grinning at Logan. He took the picnic basket Logan carried. "I'll put this in the trunk."

Tess leaned her head against the cushion and sighed. She looked over and smiled at Logan when he climbed into the back seat beside her.

"Logan, I'll drop you off at your car on the way, then take Tess home."

"Thanks, Gordon, but I'd like Logan to take me home." She glanced at him, and it seemed to him that she tried to send him a silent message.

Logan nodded. "Be happy to."

"Sounds like a plan."

"I'd like to sit with her for a little while and make sure she's okay." Logan held his breath, wondering if he was overstepping his bounds, but Tess said nothing.

"But we can—"

"Gordon, let Logan take care of her," Kathy interrupted him.

Logan saw the older man look at him in the rear-view mirror. Gordon was frowning.

Then Gordon nodded. "Fine. No use arguing with strong-minded women."

Kathy laughed. "'Bout time you realized that."

"Aunt Kathy?" Tess spoke up suddenly. "Thank you for getting groceries for me and putting dinner in my fridge."

"You're welcome, honey. It was no trouble. Gordon and I dropped it off on our way to a movie."

A few minutes later, Logan helped Tess into his car and they waved goodbye to her aunt and uncle. He set the picnic basket in the back seat and climbed into the car.

"I'm sorry to take up more of your time," Tess said as he drove them to her house.

"Don't you dare say that."

"Well, I know the last hour hasn't been pleasant for you."

"I'm sure it was worse for you."

She nodded. "I guess so."

He pulled into her driveway, cut off the engine, and tried to get out and around to her side to help her but she was already out of the car. Woman was just too independent, he thought as he reached into the back seat for the picnic basket. She seemed fully recovered, though.

Once inside, she sank onto the sofa. "Oh, it's so good to be home."

"I'll put the leftovers in the refrigerator."

"Thanks. Is there any tea left?"

"Yeah. I'll bring you a glass."

When he returned, she was lying on her side. The quilt draped on the back of the sofa was now tucked around her. He set the glass on the coffee table before her, then sat down in the chair beside the sofa.

"Logan, what happened?"

"What do you mean?"

She frowned, pulled off the elastic band that she'd used to make her hair into a ponytail, and tossed it on the table. "I don't know, some of it's a blur," she said after a moment. "I felt so weird just before I started throwing up. And I remember you asking me if I'd taken anything . . . if I was on something."

Here it came. Logan ran his hands through his hair and didn't look away from her direct stare. "I'm sorry. I had to ask."

She sat up and pulled the quilt around her shoulders. "You can't think I do drugs."

"No, Tess. You'd be the last person I'd think did that."

"Because we could never work together if you thought that," she said. "You know that. We have to be able to trust each other."

She flopped back onto the sofa and put her arm over her eyes. "Well, I know I didn't, but it sure felt like something was wrong. That wasn't like any motion sickness I've ever had."

"The doctor told me he could run some tests, but he thought it was just a bad case of motion sickness. If it was food poisoning, you wouldn't have started feeling better."

"And if it was food poisoning, you'd have gotten sick, too."

He nodded. "Why don't you drink your tea and then try to get some rest?"

"Strange afternoon."

"You got that right."

She finished the tea, lay back down, and almost instantly fell asleep. Logan watched her and thought about how he'd felt holding her in his arms.

11

Have you always been like this?"

Logan shuffled through some folders on his desk and pulled out a paper. "Like what?" He got up, walked over to the photocopier, and made some copies.

"A soft touch. An easy mark." She paused. "A sucker."

"As I remember it, you bought more boxes of Girl Scout cookies than I did." He shuffled the folders on his desk, shoved them in a drawer, and locked it. "C'mon, we're gonna go look for a dog."

She logged out of her computer and stood. "Since when are we Animal Control?"

"They're looking, too. I got a call while you were sneaking that candy bar the high school girl was selling for the homeless shelter fundraiser."

"I did not sneak a candy bar. I'm a grown woman. If I want a candy bar, I'll have one."

"Yeah, right. I saw you sneaking Girl Scout cookies earlier."

"Thin Mints are addictive," she muttered. "Someone oughta be arrested for inventing them. And even if I bought more boxes than you did, you've bought everything else. Tickets for pancake breakfasts and spaghetti suppers and sponsorships for charity walks. I bet every parent in this building knows they can come to you with some fundraiser and out comes your wallet."

"I bet I know everyone in this building already, and I've only been here for a few weeks."

He had her there. In a very short time, he'd met nearly everyone and had made friends with several men. He was even playing on the department basketball league.

"So what did you buy this time?" she asked curiously. "I saw Ed talking to you and money exchanged hands."

He pulled two tickets from his shirt pocket and waved them at her. "Maybe I'll take someone else."

She snatched at the tickets. "What are they for? A charity ball? That chocolate benefit?"

"Something even better. The historical society event."

Tess stopped dead in her tracks. "You want to go on a tour of the local cemeteries?"

"Why not? I've just seen some from a distance since I got here, and they look interesting. Besides, it's for a good cause, right?"

Laughing, she shook her head and followed him to the car. "Right. I just didn't picture you as the type to be interested in that sort of thing."

"I love history."

"History we've got," she said. "And ghost stories galore."

"So, you going to go with me?" he asked. "Be my ghoulfriend?"

She rolled her eyes, but she nodded. "I'll go with you."

By mutual agreement, they lowered the windows in the car. Fall was finally on its way after a long, hot summer. Volunteers were unloading a truckload of pumpkins at the church on the corner.

"We don't have time to stop," she warned. "And what do you need a pumpkin for, anyway?"

"Spoilsport. I was thinking we could take one to Mrs. Ramsey."

She softened. "That's nice of you to think of her."

They'd made two more trips to check for break-ins at her house. Feeling restless, she tapped her notepad on her knee.

"I'm thinking we should do another canvas of the neighbors around Toni's house."

"Good idea."

"You don't sound like you think it's a good idea. What's the matter?"

"How many times can we question people and go over our notes and the evidence? We haven't had any new leads in weeks. We're stalled."

"That's the way it is sometimes."

"I don't have your patience."

"Yes, you do, or you wouldn't have pursued Sam's case for so long." He shrugged. "I'm not feeling particularly patient." He pulled into the driveway of the house. "Let's take another walk-through of the house."

Maria had told them the house was going back to the bank next month. She'd been there going through her sister's things, boxing them up, and doing some cleaning.

Tess looked into a box sitting on the kitchen counter. Tupperware containers. She felt an instant stab of guilt. She hadn't returned the ones her aunt had used to pack the picnic food. People got really attached to their Tupperware, and her aunt was no exception. She might have thought it was a little nutty, but Aunt Kathy had told her Oprah's aunt had once claimed her niece had come asking for the containers she'd brought over for a family dinner. Tess made a mental note to take the containers to her aunt the next day when she went to her quilting class.

She walked into the living room and found Logan standing there near the spot where Toni's body was discovered.

"Let's do a last canvas of the immediate neighbors," he said. "Why don't you take the neighbor to the right, I'll take the one to the left."

Tess knocked at the door of her interview but the woman, an elderly retired nurse, didn't remember anything more than she had the afternoon Tess had talked to her.

Logan had more luck. "No new information, but I thanked him for calling Animal Control about the missing Chihuahua he saw hanging around the neighborhood a few days after the murder. He didn't have any luck getting close enough to catch him."

"Maria would be glad to have him found," Tess said. "I think it would be like having a little of her sister back."

"Well, maybe we'll get lucky today."

They drove around the neighborhood keeping an eye out for Paco. Tess saw a few posters Maria had put up on utility poles.

"There's a convenience store around the corner. Let's go in there and ask if they've seen Paco."

"Good idea."

Tess carried the poster in, showed her badge to the clerk, and asked him if he'd seen the dog. Logan went to the self-serve drink machine for sweet tea.

"Hey, that's the dog the homeless guy brought in a little while ago," the clerk said. "I told him no dogs were allowed, but he said it was too hot to leave him outside. I gave in, said he could bring him in if he carried him."

She pulled out her notepad. "Can you describe him?"

"The dog or the man?" the clerk asked, chuckling.

Logan set the drinks on the counter. "The man, wise guy."

The clerk's smile faded. He looked at Tess. "He with you?"

"Yeah. He's got a badge and everything."

"He might still be hanging around out back. Sometimes he takes a rest back there."

"So he's in the neighborhood on a regular basis?"

The clerk took Logan's money and rang up the sale. "Yeah. For maybe the last four or five months."

So they walked out of the store and around back.

And Tess nearly tripped over the man with the Chihuahua sitting on his lap.

Logan didn't know who was more startled—the humans or the Chihuahua when they encountered each other.

Paco the Chihuahua jumped up on the man's lap and began growling.

"Shh, it's okay, buddy," he said, soothing the dog and holding it when the dog tried to lunge forward.

"Careful," Logan cautioned and reached for Tess's arm to keep her from going forward quickly and getting herself bitten.

The man got to his feet with some effort—holding the dog as well as a dilapidated knapsack that had seen better days. Logan judged him to be in his forties, but he looked older with the inevitable windburn and sunburn Logan noticed on the homeless in this part of the country. He must have been out in the elements for some time.

"Buddy here won't hurt you," he said. "He's just scared."

"I'm Logan, and this is Tess," he told the man. "What's your name?"

"Jim," the man said with a touch of belligerence.

"Jim, where did you get the dog?" Tess asked quietly.

"He's mine," the man asserted.

"You're sure?"

"Finders keepers," the man said, backing down a little. "I saw him wandering around the neighborhood for several days. If someone owns him, they need to take care of him. It's not easy being on the streets."

Logan nodded. "You're right. No one should let their dog roam the streets. But we think we know who the dog belongs to, and they didn't let the dog out. Someone else did. We'd like to ask you some questions."

"I haven't done anything wrong. You can't arrest me for just being homeless."

"We're not," Logan said quietly, standing still, and not making any sudden moves to alarm the man or the dog. "We just want to ask you some questions."

"Be right back," Tess said, backing away.

He nodded, not looking at her. He didn't think the man was armed, but he'd learned not to make assumptions.

Tess was back in no time, holding a hot dog from the convenience store. She broke off a bite and offered it cautiously to the dog.

From the way the man watched the process, Logan could make one assumption: the man hadn't eaten in a while. He glanced at Tess, and she nodded. After she fed the dog half of the hot dog, she wrapped it back up.

"It's awfully hot out here," Tess said. "Not good for man or dog. Let's go take care of those questions and get out of the sun."

She held out her arms. "Can Paco ride with me?"

"Paco? That's his name?"

Tess nodded. "Someone's been frantic worrying about him. She'll be so grateful you took care of him."

The man handed Paco to Tess, and Logan was relieved to see that the dog was licking her fingers instead of biting them, his tail wagging madly.

"Logan and I are way past due for lunch," she told Jim. "We'll stop and get something on the way. Tell me what kind of sub and drink we can get you."

The man drew himself up. "You don't need to feel sorry for me."

"Jim, were you raised in the South?"

"Yeah, why?"

"Then you know we don't eat in front of someone without offering him some of what we're having."

She shot a look at Logan. "Even though he's a Yankee, I bet Logan was raised the same way."

The man studied her for a moment, then grinned. "Okay. Ham and cheese and a root beer?"

"Sounds good. We'll meet you there soon as we pick up the food."

She signaled and a marked car pulled up. "Don't worry, Officer Graham here is just giving you a ride into the station for questioning. He has to make sure you don't have any weapons, okay?"

Jim held up his hands and submitted to the check. "I carry a pocketknife."

"Lots of men in these parts do," she said, nodding. "You grow up a boy in the South you have to have a pocketknife for fishing and hunting. Don't know what boys in Chicago carry. Logan? Brass knuckles?"

"Very funny," Logan told her. He waited until Jim, then Graham got into the car and drove away, before he started around the store to their car. "What's your impression?"

"We have a problem with the homeless here just like other cities," Tess told him as she got into the car. "But you know the homeless don't commit violent crimes any more than the rest of the population. Let's face it, when you're trying to take care of basic needs you don't have much time to plot out a crime."

They drove to a sub shop, picked up three foot-longs and drinks, and continued on to the station.

The minute they walked into the station Maria came rushing toward them, tears streaming down her face. "Paco! You found him!"

Logan watched Tess struggle to hold the dog and keep him from flying out of her arms. She gave Maria the dog and then stood back, blinking hard as she watched Maria cry over the dog.

Could dogs cry? Logan wondered. It sure looked like Paco had tears in his eyes.

He must need his own eyes examined, he told himself.

Maria turned and thanked them before she hurried down the hallway. A moment later they heard high-pitched, frantic barking, and a familiar voice bellowing to restrain the dog and get it out of the station.

"That's Gordon," Tess said and hurried down the hall.

Logan followed her, carrying the subs and drinks. They found Maria holding Paco as Gordon backed away and went into one of the interrogation rooms and slammed the door.

"I don't know what got into Paco," Maria said, trying to soothe the dog.

"Shh, Paco," Tess said and she reached into her pocket for the portion of the hot dog left from earlier. "I'm sure he's just a little unsettled about everything being so different."

The dog quickly scarfed down the rest of the hot dog. Tess looked at Maria. "I hope he doesn't get sick from this, but I got it for him earlier."

"He can barf all over the seat of my car for all I care." Maria kissed the top of the dog's head. "I'm going to go ask my boss if I can get off early and take him home."

Tess opened the door of the interrogation room since Logan's hands were full with lunch. He put the food down on the table.

"Hi, Gordon," Logan said. "I didn't realize that you were joining us. Have you had lunch?"

"Yes, thanks. But I'm not joining you. I was just keeping Jim company until you two got here."

He stood. "See y'all around."

Logan sat and watched Jim watch Gordon leave the room. Jim's forehead appeared beaded with sweat when it hadn't been as he sat out behind the convenience store. His hands trembled as he popped the top of his root beer and took a deep swallow.

"I swear, I'm always thirsty here," Logan said as he popped the top of his own Coke. "All this sun dehydrates me."

Tess popped the top of her Diet Coke and pulled out her notepad. "Better to sweat than to freeze, right, Jim? You couldn't pay me enough to live someplace like Logan's beloved Chicago."

Logan handed Jim his sandwich. "But you just don't have decent deep-dish pizza here. If you had that, I'd think this place was perfect." He paused. "Go ahead and eat, Jim."

The man tucked the sandwich into his backpack. "I'll save it for later, if you don't mind."

"If you want," Logan said. "But we'll be happy to drop you off at St. Francis House or one of the other homeless shelters if you'd like."

"Look, let's get down to brass tacks, shall we?" Jim said in a weary voice. "It's all well and good to be nice to me, but you brought me here for a reason."

Logan and Tess exchanged a look. "We brought you here to ask how you came to have the dog," Logan said.

"I found him. I didn't steal him. He was hanging around a block or so from the convenience store. When he saw me sit down with a sandwich, he came over and wanted to be friends. So I've had him ever since."

And no matter what they asked him, he stuck to that story. Logan showed him a photo of Toni and asked if he knew her. Jim said he didn't. Tess hammered at him about why he was in that neighborhood, and Jim said he sometimes slept in a shed at the rear of a home empty because of foreclosure.

Tess excused herself when she got a call she had to take, and Logan let Jim take a break. They both drank from their cans of soda but neither of them touched their sandwiches.

When Tess returned, she gestured for him to step out into the hallway and he did so, closing the door behind him.

"Time to cut him loose, don't you think? I don't believe this is our man."

He nodded. "Let's do that, and we'll talk."

Jim looked up when they walked back into the room.

"Thanks for talking with us," Logan said.

He laughed, but the sound was rusty and humorless. "Like I had any choice."

"An officer's going to take you wherever you like," Logan told him.

Tess held out an envelope. "This is a little something for taking care of the dog."

Jim stood and lifted his chin. "I told you I didn't want your charity."

"It isn't charity, and it isn't from me," she said quietly. "You kept the dog safe and it means a lot to the woman we reunited Paco with. You see, her sister was murdered and the dog ran away. Having the dog back makes the woman feel like she can still do something for her sister."

Jim went still. "I didn't know."

Tess nodded. "We could tell. So take her gift in the spirit it's intended, Jim. It would mean a lot to her."

He took the envelope and tucked it in his pocket. Then he looked at Logan. "I'd like that ride to the shelter after all."

Logan gestured for him to precede him out the door and introduced him to an officer, then returned to the interrogation room. "Let's go eat our lunch someplace else. I'd like to be out of this room, if you don't mind."

"I don't mind at all," she agreed.

But before they could gather up their subs, Gordon stuck his head in the door. "Did one of you ask that the homeless guy get a ride?"

"I did," Logan said. "Problem?"

"You brought him in for questioning in a murder case, and you're mollycoddling him with a ride?"

"I wouldn't call a ride to a shelter 'mollycoddling', but, yes, I did ask an officer to give Jim a courtesy ride."

"I don't see the point of giving the homeless treatment like that," Gordon returned. "There's a man who's panhandling instead of working, and even if he didn't murder someone, no telling what he's been up to."

"I figure we should see someone we asked to come in for questioning taken wherever they want to go," Logan told him. "We should care about their safety as well as anyone else's."

"What's one homeless person more or less?" He turned on his heel to stride away.

Tess looked mortified. She walked over and shut the door, and then turned to Logan. "I'd have spoken up, but it does no good with him. Gordon's like a lot of people. He thinks he has reasons for his opinion, and there's no changing him."

"Didn't you tell me he and your aunt go to your church?"

"Oh, he's one of the board members," she said with a tight smile. "Since when did church attendance mean someone's a good Christian?"

"Amen," he muttered. "Come on, let's go eat these outside somewhere. I could use some fresh air."

12

Tess watched Logan hand over their tickets outside the Huguenot Cemetery. The cemetery was the oldest in the area and that was saying a lot since St. Augustine was more than four hundred years old.

She was used to showing people around who visited her from another state. Florida was pretty much known as the "drop-in" state. Residents got used to out-of-state family or friends wanting to visit and stay, maybe take in a visit to see Mickey Mouse over in Orlando.

Logan seemed to embrace his new city with a passion, wanting to know more about its history.

Dusk was falling and with it, temperatures were dropping. She'd brought a sweater just in case, although she didn't think she'd need it. She'd also brought bug spray, and she knew without a doubt they'd need that.

Logan slapped at his arm. "Geez, the mosquitoes are as big as pelicans."

She pulled the bug spray from her purse and handed it to him. "Imagine not having something like this back in the 'good old days.'"

When they got there, a small group had already assembled at the cemetery located near the old city gates. Tess thought it was interesting that the city's welcome center had been located next to the cemetery; so many visitors made a point of visiting its historic cemeteries.

"I don't believe in ghosts," she whispered.

"Me neither. But this is supposed to be something a little different about the people who were the first residents of the city."

"And the tickets were being sold for a good cause," she said tongue-in-cheek.

The tour guide began telling them about how the cemetery opened so those who weren't Catholic had a place for burial. An outbreak of yellow fever had struck St. Augustine, so another cemetery became necessary .

A woman appeared in the long, flowing dress of the French Huguenots—the French Protestants—of the sixteenth century. She spoke of the horrors of entire families wiped out by the terrible disease as others watched helplessly.

Survivor guilt. That's what she'd heard it called. Tess glanced up at the lighthouse peeking through the trees. It was all well and good to say she didn't believe in ghosts, but in a way, Sam's death had haunted her. One afternoon when she'd been grieving, she'd gone for a walk on her campus. She'd found herself at the student center talking to a counselor. The woman had listened and told Tess she wasn't just grieving for her friend—that she was experiencing survivor's guilt.

It made sense. Too much sense. She and Sam had switched dresses that night, and Tess had wondered if the killer meant to kill her instead of Sam.

"If this is going to make you sad, we'll go," Logan said.

She dragged her attention back to the present. "No, it's fine. I was just thinking of something."

"Some*one*," he corrected "Sam?"

She nodded.

A man in the formal dress of the 1880s introduced himself as Judge John B. Stickney. He sat on a tall gravestone, regarded them solemnly, and then began to talk. The tour members chuckled as he dispensed legal advice to a couple he chose from the group.

They moved on to another cemetery a few short blocks away. "When we were kids, we called it the Tomato Cemetery," Tess whispered to Logan. "We couldn't pronounce Tolomato."

A man dressed as a Franciscan monk came out to talk about converting the Indians to Christianity, and how the cemetery was a final resting place for former slaves who fled bondage in the Carolinas. Ed, a fellow officer, stepped forward and talked of freedom and raising his family here—children who helped build the city.

"I didn't know he was going to be in this," Tess whispered to Logan.

"Me, neither," he whispered.

As Ed walked past them, he winked at them.

Then a woman stepped forward and talked of walking seventy miles to ask for refuge from the British governor who ruled over St. Augustine. "I am from Minorca, an island in the Mediterranean," she said proudly, her voice ringing out as the group stood, enthralled. "We came to this country as indentured servants, promising to work to pay our passage. But we were enslaved, worked like animals, until we fell in the fields south of here. Governor Tonyn granted us refuge, and some of us lie here now in these grounds."

"That concludes our tour," the tour leader said. "I hope you enjoyed it."

The group applauded the volunteers and then dispersed, chatting about dinner and shopping.

"So what do you think of our town?" Tess asked Logan.

He reached for her hand and she let him take it.

"I think I like it a lot," he said. "Want to walk a little more? It's such a beautiful night."

She nodded and they strolled down the street. A car pulled up beside them and Tess glanced over.

"Playing tourist?" Pete Orman, one of their fellow officers, called through the open window.

Logan grinned and waved. "She's showing me around."

The radio squawked, and the officer's attention was immediately riveted.

"Break-in," Tess murmured when she heard the code. "I know that address. Potter's Wax Museum. Pete, we'll go with you."

The lock clicked open on the car doors.

Pete radioed in two off-duty officers were joining him, and then they were off, speeding down the narrow city streets to the museum.

"I've been here so many times," Tess told them. "We were always coming here for school field trips. I know the place like the back of my hand."

She turned to Logan. "Kids like to break in for a prank, steal something like a prop. Sometimes break off a finger and show it off at school."

They listened to the dispatcher report that the K-9 officer was on the trail of a hit-and-run driver. He'd be sent as soon as he became available.

"I'll go in and check it out," Tess decided. "Could be a faulty alarm."

"You don't have a radio," Pete pointed out.

She pulled out her cell phone and set it to vibrate. "You do the same," she told Logan. "That way I can let you know if there's any problem. Don't come in or you could get your kneecaps shot at. Or worse," she said with emphasis.

"I've seen her on the firing range," Pete said. "You want to listen to her about that." He glanced at Tess. "You take the flashlight since you're going inside."

Tess nodded and reached for her weapon tucked in her purse. She was out the door the moment Pete stopped the car in the parking lot.

Sure enough, the back door bore marks of tampering. The three of them noted it, looked at each other and signaled Pete would walk around the building to the left, Logan to the right.

Tess went in, holding her gun in a defensive stance.

Most of the lights were out. The interior of the museum looked dim and eerie. Tess moved slowly, going by memory rather than turning on the flashlight in her left hand and alerting anyone who might still be inside.

Quiet had its own sound. She heard a faint hum of traffic outside. But as much as she strained to hear the sound of breathing or a footfall or the creak of a floorboard there was nothing.

Tess turned a corner and a line of figures she could recognize as presidents caught her attention. Their eyes followed her as she walked past, squinting to make sure a real man didn't stand among them. President Clinton smiled toothily at her, almost making her smile back. Funny, President Lincoln seemed shorter than he had when she visited as a middle schooler. Well, she'd grown quite a bit since then.

Kings and queens held court, with Henry the Eighth seeming to leer as she passed. Marie Antoinette looked pale, beautiful, and haughty as ever in her sumptuous dress of silk, lace, and velvet.

She felt a sneeze coming on. Marie hadn't sent her dress out to for cleaning in at least a century or two. Tess tucked the flashlight under her left arm and ruthlessly squeezed her nose. She moved faster, her eyes sweeping from one side of the room to another.

The figures of Hollywood film stars stood waiting for their fans but no human stood with them. Tess walked into the exhibit of film villains and felt chills creep over her skin. Her heart beat faster as she moved past Freddy and Dracula. She froze and her fingers tightened on her gun. Had the scythe held by the Grim Reaper moved?

She shook her head. Imagination was getting the best of her. The cell phone vibrated, her signal to check in with Logan. She stepped into a room of European historical figures, backed into a corner, and pulled out the phone. Hiding the lighted dial with one hand, she hit speed dial for Logan, a silent signal faster than texting, then broke the connection since she couldn't talk inside the building. She couldn't be sure the burglar wasn't still in the building.

Then she saw the rose on the floor. She bent to pick it up, certain she'd find it was a silk one from the vase of flowers near Lucretia Borgia, the medieval poisoner. But the rose was a fresh one, felt dewy against her nose, and smelled divine.

She looked up into the proud, arrogant face of Machiavelli. Something stirred in her memory, something someone had said. Frowning, she moved past him and on down the hall to the back door.

Tess walked out just as Logan punched in the speed dial to call her again.

Mixed emotions rose up in him. He wanted to shake her for making him worry; he wanted to kiss her and hold her and know that she was all right.

He could do neither with the officer standing there beside him.

She holstered her weapon and looked at Pete. "I can't say for sure no one's in there—it's just too full of hiding places."

"K-9's on the way," he told her. "Thanks, Tess, Logan. Sorry you had your evening interrupted. Want a ride back to your car?"

"We'll walk," Logan told him without waiting for Tess to speak.

He turned and began walking.

"Wait up!" Tess called, but he ignored her. "Hey!" she said as she caught up with him. "Something wrong?"

Logan glared at her and then focused on the road ahead of him. "How would you have felt if I'd gone in there and you'd been outside waiting, wondering what was going on?"

"Oh, no, now you're doing it too, are you?" she snapped bitterly. "What was I supposed to do, stand outside, and let the man go in? Shake my hands and cry, 'My, my!'"

He stopped, and she nearly ran into him. "Don't be ridiculous!"

"Oh, now I'm ridiculous?" Her eyes blazed at him as she stood, her hands on her hips.

"I don't think of you as a woman when we're at work!" he snapped. "You're my partner!"

Before he could stop himself, he grasped her arms and stared down into her shocked eyes. "It's all the other hours of the day I think of you I'm worried about."

He kissed her, wrapping his arms around her, and holding her tight so she couldn't get away from him.

But she didn't try. Instead, she seemed to melt against him, returning his kiss, and threading her fingers through his hair.

Someone whistled, and there was laughter.

They pulled apart. She looked as shocked as he did, and they backed away at the same time.

"Wow," slipped out before he could stop himself.

She avoided looking at him, walking quickly away.

"Hey, buddy, she dropped this," a man said and held out the rose Tess had been carrying when she walked out of the museum.

Logan took it, thanking the man absently, then he shook his head and hurried after her.

"Where'd this come from?" he asked when he caught up with her. He held out the rose, she took it from him, but wouldn't look at him.

"I found it inside the museum, lying on the floor. It didn't seem to be part of any display around it."

"You were picking up flowers inside the museum."

She frowned. "Yeah, so?"

"While I was outside, sweating bullets about you being inside with who knows what kind of person that broke into a building." It was a statement, not a question.

"I don't like your tone."

"Yeah, well, live with it!"

"You wouldn't be talking like this if I were a man!"

"I wouldn't have kissed you if you were a man!"

"There you are, thinking about me like I'm a woman again!" She threw up her hands and stomped away.

Logan clasped his head in his hands and then, when he saw how fast her long strides were carrying her away from him, he hurried after her.

"Tess, do you hear what you're saying?"

She just glared at him as they came to stand beside his car.

Logan fumbled in his pocket for his keys, unlocked the car, and they got in. "I don't know what to say," he told her finally. "I didn't intend to become attracted to you. We're partners.

That's a delicate relationship at best. But I can't deny having feelings for you and from the way you kissed me back, we know you have some for me as well."

She sighed. "If anyone at work knew—"

Logan pulled into her driveway. "It's no one else's business at this point." He reached for her hand and when she resisted, he pulled his back and sighed. "You are the most capable police officer I've ever worked with," he said quietly. "Officer. Not female officer. But Tess, I really like the woman, and I want to get to know her as well."

He watched the play of emotion on her face.

"I have to go," she said finally. "I'll—I'll talk to you later." She unbuckled her seat belt and got out of the car. Then she leaned down and looked at him. "I had a good time. Thanks."

With that, she left him, walking up to her front door, and letting herself into the house. He sat there drumming his fingers on the steering wheel for a long moment, and then he backed out of the driveway and turned toward home.

13

Tess rubbed at her eyes and put the lighthouse quilt down for a moment.

She hadn't slept well, and when her neighbor had woken her early mowing his lawn, she'd gotten up, fixed a cup of coffee, and took the quilt out onto the front porch. She sat in a big old weather-beaten wicker chair she couldn't bear to throw away. It creaked as she sat there stitching on the quilt.

Fall was in the air. She could smell the difference in it. Few trees changed color here, so the signs of fall were harder to spot. It was more a difference in the muggy smell of air and a drop in temperature that signaled the change of season.

Fred next door knew. The dachshund sat on his porch deeply sniffing the air. Tess smiled as she sipped her coffee.

A car pulled into her driveway. Logan. He got out, reached into the back seat, and she saw he'd bought a huge pumpkin. It must have weighed a ton but he carried it easily, climbed the steps, and set it down.

"Peace offering."

She raised her brows. "I've never been brought a pumpkin for a peace offering."

"I brought some flowers, too, but I thought I'd get this out first."

"Flowers will be a comedown after a pumpkin."

"Yeah, I thought so, too. Maybe I'll just leave them in the car."

"Don't you dare!"

She watched him walk out to the car and return with a pot of golden mums. "Pretty. Thank you." She gestured at the wicker sofa. "Have a seat."

He sat, stretching out his long jeans-clad legs. "Is that what you've been working on in your classes?"

She nodded. "I've never done one like this before. Want some coffee?"

"I can get it. Don't get up." He paused on his way inside. "Want some more?"

"I better not. This is my second cup."

He went inside and returned with a mug. "Why a lighthouse?"

Tess ran a hand over the quilt, then looked up at him with a frown. "I don't know. I just felt like I needed to do it."

She pulled quilt blocks from the tote bag sitting beside her and moved them around on her lap. So far she'd made several: one was a sailboat, another a picnic table with a lunch spread out on a cloth, another children playing on the grounds. Another, a couple standing at the top of the lighthouse, looking out at the view. Her favorite was the one she'd designed of a girl in an old-fashioned blue gown with a billowy long skirt.

Blue. She stopped and a memory washed over her . . . Sam twirling around in her blue prom dress, her shoulders wrapped in a lacy summer shawl.

"Tess?"

She shook her head and came back to today. "I suppose going over the case made me think about it. The lighthouse, I mean."

She leaned back in her chair and looked out at the neighborhood. "I told you that Sam worked there. She loved the lighthouse and loved showing it to visitors. In a way, I'm not surprised she was found there. She would have felt safe on the grounds."

"It may be the killer is trying to tell us that," he said quietly. "She felt safe with whoever she went there with or whoever she met there. She knew them. Even if she was upset with weasel Wendell, would she have gone there at night by herself? Was it just an opportunity killing? One where she just happened to be there? I kind of doubt it, don't you?" He paused. "Are all the squares—what do you call them?"

"Quilt blocks."

"Are those all part of some pattern?"

"No, I designed them. Why?"

Logan set his mug down and leaned over to study them. "How did you decide what blocks you want?"

She smiled at him. "You don't have to show interest in this. Most men aren't interested in quilting."

He met her gaze. "I don't play those games. I'm interested in what you're interested in. But I have a reason for asking. I'm wondering if you're using this as a problem-solving technique. If you're using it to puzzle out some aspect of the crime."

"I wondered that myself."

"You look tired."

"Gee, thanks. Just what a girl wants to hear."

"If it's any consolation, I didn't sleep well, either. I don't like it that we argued." He reached over, and this time, she took his hand.

"I don't either."

"Truce?"

"Truce."

"Listen, do you have plans? If you don't, I thought we could take a drive, have some lunch."

"I don't have plans until later."

"Later?"

"The barbecue at my aunt and Gordon's. You were invited, remember? Everyone at work was."

"I wasn't sure if I'd go."

She gave him a direct look. "Because of last night?"

He shrugged. "Didn't want you to be uncomfortable."

"I see. Well, I wouldn't have been and there's no reason now, right?"

"Right. So I guess I'm going."

"Anyway, my only plan for today was to make a quick visit to Mrs. Ramsey. So if you don't mind, I want to do it before we go to lunch. It won't take long. I stop in every couple weeks when I have a Saturday off."

"She's a nice lady. I wouldn't mind at all. Are you sure she won't mind me coming with you?"

Tess shook her head and began putting her quilting pieces back in her tote bag. "She seemed to like you."

She happened to glance in the backseat of the car as she got in. There was another big pumpkin and a pot of mums sitting on the back seat.

Curiosity killed her, but she wasn't going to ask who they were for. When Logan glanced over at her, she pretended she hadn't been looking, but she figured he'd noticed when she saw the smile playing around his lips.

When they got out of the car at Mrs. Ramsey's, he reached into the back seat and hefted the pumpkin in his arms. "Will you get the flowers?"

"Sure."

"Now I'm glad I got extra. They had a good sale and you know, it was—"

"For a good cause," she finished.

He grinned. "Yeah."

"Why, what a nice surprise!" Mrs. Ramsey said when she opened the door. "And look what you've brought!"

"These are from Logan," Tess told her as she set the pot of flowers down on a table on the porch.

"Where shall I put this?" he asked.

Mrs. Ramsey pointed to the wide concrete edging on the porch. "Let's put it over here, where people can see it from the street. Thank you so much, Logan. That was very sweet."

When they went inside, she insisted on making them tea. Logan carried the tray out to the living room, and she hurried to move the newspaper from the coffee table so he could set it down.

"Mmm, these are so good," he said as he popped the last of the second cookie into his mouth. "You should go into business. Mrs. Fields would go broke."

She laughed and shook her head. "I just use the recipe on the back of the tollhouse morsels."

"Mine never turn out as good," Tess told him.

They chatted about the changing weather, Mrs. Ramsey's grandchildren, Logan's adjustment to the city and the job.

Then Tess leaned forward. "Mrs. Ramsey, tell me about Machiavelli."

Machiavelli?

Logan had been sitting there, mellowing out on some of the best chocolate chip cookies he'd ever eaten, enjoying a leisurely Saturday off, when Tess brought up the wax museum.

A couple chocolate chips lodged in his throat, and he coughed as he remembered the argument from the previous night. He reached for his tea and washed them down. "That the guy you found the rose near last night?"

Tess nodded and looked at Mrs. Ramsey. "There was a break-in at the wax museum last night. I went in and just as I was leaving I found a rose near a figure of Machiavelli."

"Ah, Niccolo di Bernardo dei Machiavelli," Mrs. Ramsey said. "Fifteenth-century Italian politician in the time of the Medici family. Fascinating man. His very name has come to represent manipulation and political machinations."

She picked up the plate of cookies and offered them to Tess, then Logan.

"We didn't study his writing in the English class you took with me," she told Tess. "He's usually studied in college—not just in literature classes but political science classes. He's best known for writing *The Prince* and *The Art of War*."

"I read that in college," Logan remembered. "*The Prince*. As I remember it, he believed that the ends justified the means, that—" he stopped as there was loud banging on the front door and then a key turned in the lock.

"Gramma!" a child shouted, and a small whirlwind in pigtails and a pink tutu ran into the room.

Cats scattered to the four corners of the house.

Mrs. Ramsey grinned and held out her arms. "Katie-kins! There's my grandgirl!"

A young woman walked in and smiled. "Sorry, there's no restraining her. Hi, Tess."

"Hi, Lindsey. This is Logan. Logan, Lindsey graduated two years before me and works as a nurse."

"Becoming a nurse was good training for having kids," Lindsey said as she reached for a cookie. "Between Katie and my son, Mark, I spend a lot of time taking care of scrapes and boo-boos."

Tess stood and bent to hug Mrs. Ramsey. "We just stopped by for a few minutes. We'll let you visit with your family."

"Don't let us chase you off," Lindsey protested. "Katie, do NOT pull Jezebel's tail or you're going to get scratched."

Katie put her hands behind her back and tried to look innocent.

"We're not letting you chase us off," Tess assured Lindsey. "Logan and I have plans."

Logan took Tess's lead and got to his feet. Mrs. Ramsey held out her arms to him and they hugged.

"Thank you both for the pumpkin and the flowers."

"Our pleasure," he said. He saw the warm smile Tess sent him.

"Can we make a jack-o-lantern, Gramma?" he heard Katie ask as they walked to the door.

They stopped at a seafood place for lunch and sat on the deck for a while and listened to a man who sang about summer fading fast. The day was beautiful, so the tourists were out. "I thought we could take a drive down A1A, the ocean highway."

"Sounds good."

There wasn't a cloud in the sky as they drove. The ocean spread out to their left, a beautiful aquamarine.

"They don't have that in Chicago," Tess told him.

Logan grinned at her. "I know. I hope you don't take this for granted."

Tess pulled the band from her hair and let it blow in the breeze coming in the window. "Never. I wouldn't trade it for anything."

"Do we have time to walk on the beach for a few minutes?"

"Sure."

Logan parked, and they walked down the stairs over the dunes to the sand below. He took off his Dockers, and Tess kicked off her flip-flops. It felt a little strange to feel the warm sand beneath his feet and the sun on his shoulders. He wondered how long it would be before this stopped feeling like a vacation place and just felt like home.

Sandpipers skittered along the edge of the water, darting back and forth as the waves splashed at their feet. A seagull cried as it circled over a family sitting on a blanket and eating. A little boy threw a crust of bread, and the gull caught it neatly in its beak.

The sand was a pinkish color here. Logan bent to scoop up a handful to look at it.

"It's mixed with crushed coquina, a soft stone, here in Flagler Beach," she told him. "It's a different composition than up at St. Augustine beach."

They walked for a time, and then Tess dropped to the soft, dry sand near a clump of tall, waving sea oats. "I'm so tired," she complained. "Not enough sleep. Too much sun. Too much lunch."

He sat next to her and watched the waves with her and wondered when was the last time he'd felt so peaceful. A few minutes later, he felt himself smiling when she leaned against him, her head on his shoulder. Then he realized she was sleeping. He'd never seen her so relaxed. Something relaxed in him, too; they'd gotten past what had happened the night before or she couldn't be as relaxed with him.

The waves rolled in, then out, a timeless rhythm. Sitting here, staring at the vast expanse of the ocean, made him wonder at the bigger picture. He'd been angry at God for taking his friend, a little depressed at the emptiness he felt after the big case was solved—it had given him something to focus his anger on for a long time. He'd felt driven . . . and then there was no place to put all that anger and effort.

He'd thought he'd come here for the challenge of solving another big case, but gradually this woman had gotten under his skin. And he started wanting more. He wanted some normalcy. Some pleasure in a day like this.

Maybe even a future with a woman like this.

People talked about God having a plan for their lives. He'd thought he had his own plan and hadn't ever really felt like there was some big divine plan for him.

Now he wondered.

Something was coming back to life again within him and if he knew Jason as he did, he knew he'd be happy. Just before he'd died, Jason had looked at him one day and said, "Don't take yourself so seriously. Lighten up."

The people down the beach got up, gathered up their blanket, and headed to their car. Without moving too much and waking Tess up, Logan turned his wrist and checked the time. He didn't want to wake her. She must need the rest. But she might not be happy if they were late to her aunt's party.

"Tess?" he whispered. "Time to wake up."

"Mmm?" she murmured. "What?"

He turned his head just as she lifted hers and their lips were a breath apart. He kissed her softly, not wanting to startle her, and felt her smile and respond sleepily.

"Mmm," she said. "Don't want to wake up."

And then she did, opening her eyes and staring deep into his.

14

Tess stared into Logan's eyes and felt as if she'd dropped into the deep end of the ocean.

She told herself she was having this reaction because she was half-asleep, that she was relaxed from a lovely lunch and the warm sun beating down on her head and shoulders. The waves were hypnotic.

But she knew the effect came from being near Logan. From being kissed by Logan. From his arm wrapped around her waist, holding her close.

"We need to go."

"Do we have to?" he asked, his face so close his breath whispered across her lips.

"I think we better."

With a sigh, he got to his feet and reached down to offer his hand. She took it, and he pulled her up to stand inches from him.

"Logan."

He put his hand behind her head, brought her closer, and kissed her again. "Now we can go."

Smiling, she shook her head and let him keep her hand as they walked back the way they'd come.

They stamped the sand from their feet when they got to the wooden steps up the dune and walked back to the car.

"Maybe we can come do this again next week?"

"Like the beach, huh?"

He looked at her. "I like you."

"And I like you."

"How are we going to do this?"

She started to say something, to ease the tension she suddenly felt, but the words dried up. He was looking at her so seriously and joking about it would be wrong.

"I like to keep my private life private," she told him. "I don't think it's anyone else's business if we see each other and at some point if we don't—"

"Don't project," he interrupted, tugging at her hand to stop her. "Don't talk like it's not going to work out."

"Okay," she said slowly.

He reached out to tuck a strand of her hair behind her ear. "You sure we have to go to this thing?"

"I promised I'd help Aunt Kathy with the food."

"I thought maybe you had," he said and resumed walking. "That's why I woke you up."

"It was a catnap. I'd have woken up in a minute."

He grinned at her. "Yeah."

They went to the party in separate cars, but Tess wondered if anyone would have noticed. Everyone was in the backyard already enjoying a cold drink and checking out the progress of the barbecue.

Tess brought a fresh veggie tray and pasta salad and placed them on the long table loaded with all the items her aunt and others had made.

"Hi there," Logan said as he set a grocery store bag down on the table and began unloading half a dozen containers of dips and bags of chips and snacks.

"Typical guy contribution," she teased.

"Hey, it's what's popular," he told her as several children immediately ran over to help themselves.

"So, who do you think you're fooling?" her aunt asked her when she returned to the kitchen.

"Excuse me?"

"You think arriving in separate cars really fools anyone?"

Tess rolled her eyes. "I don't know what you're talking about."

"Gordon's taking credit for matching the two of you up."

She raised her eyebrows. "Really? How does he figure he did that?"

"He brought Logan here."

Tess snatched a chicken wing her aunt was taking from a tray and piling into a basket.

"Wow, this is hot," Tess sputtered.

"You saw me just get them out of the oven."

"No, I mean it's spicy!" She grabbed a glass and poured herself some sweet tea. "Can I take those and pass them around for you?"

"Sure." Kathy handed her the basket. "Just make sure you pass them around to more than you."

"Very funny."

She offered them to Gordon first as he stood supervising several barbecue grills. "Why, thank you!" he said, and then he bit in. His eyes widened and he gaped at her. "Whoa! Foul!"

"Yeah, it's fowl," she said, pretending to misunderstand him. "It's a chicken wing."

He grabbed for a beer he'd stationed on a nearby table and took a healthy swig. "What'd I ever do to you?"

"Told Aunt Kathy you were responsible for getting Logan and me together," she said, giving him a level stare.

"Well, I did. I met him and recruited him at a conference."

"You made it sound like you were matchmaking," she said severely.

"Well, how's that going?" he asked, giving her a shameless grin.

She glared at him and walked away to offer the wings to a few other hapless victims—er, guests. Logan was next, then Smithers, and Ed. She got the same reactions she had from Gordon—cries of "Fire!" and "I need a drink!"

"Don't blame me, blame Kathy," she said with a big smile.

"I think you enjoyed that," Logan said when she set the basket down on the table.

"I'm sure I don't know what you're talking about," she responded, looking at him with wide eyes. "Are you having a good time?"

"Yeah, I am. You?"

She nodded.

Gordon clanged two barbecue tools together. "Meat's ready! Who wants a steak?"

Logan jostled Tess out of the way, as she grabbed a plate and got in line.

"Hey!"

"You're just one of the guys here, remember?" he whispered with a wicked grin. "You didn't want to let anyone think we're dating."

She just stood there and stared at him and let him have the last word.

This time.

"Logan, Tess, you two sit here!"

Logan glanced at Tess as they walked to one of the picnic tables set up in the back yard.

"I thought—"

"Just do it," Tess said as she smiled. "Objecting's just going to get noticed more."

Other couples sat next to each other. Like Noah's Ark, thought Logan. He didn't mind—he was quite happy to be sitting next to Tess. But he wondered how Tess felt about being seated with him so obviously.

Kathy looked at his plate. "Honey, did you get enough food?"

"More than."

"Well, you just remember there's more where that came from," she said, spreading a napkin over her lap. "Here in the South, we believe in making sure folks have more than enough when they sit at our table."

Tess grinned. "We know you've had enough when we have to help you push yourself away from the table."

"Detectives can eat like that," Bill Reilly said. "But I never know when I'm going to have to run after a bad guy. Gotta keep my girlish figure."

There was laughter and good-natured ribbing. Everyone called Reilly "Big Bill" because he had the stature of a running back and had just been featured in a newspaper article for running down a suspect the day before.

"Chief not coming?" someone asked.

"Got the flu," Gordon told them. He looked at Logan and Tess. "He's taking some heat from the mayor about the latest murder. Told him to tell the mayor we have our best people on it. Don't know how long that'll hold him, though."

Logan nodded. "Public officials always take the heat when we don't turn up a killer right away."

"Could we not talk about such things just one night?" Kathy said in a plaintive tone.

Gordon gave her a withering look. "You knew what you were getting into when you married a cop," he told her brusquely.

He turned to the man next to him. "Big Bill, how are you liking the sauce on those ribs?" he asked, oblivious to the fact that his wife's lips trembled and she looked ready to cry.

One of the wives started to say something, but her husband shook his head and she subsided.

"Aunt Kathy, I hope you made your Key lime pie," Tess said.

"Yes, yes I did," Kathy said.

Tess stood and picked up her plate. "Well, I'm ready for dessert. Let me help you cut that up and serve it."

Logan watched the two women walk into the house. Tess's suggestion had been so quick, so smooth, he wondered if she'd had to use such a tactic before.

"Great steak," he told Gordon.

"There's more."

He patted his stomach. "Couldn't fit one in if I tried. And that pie is sounding good on a warm night like this. Anyone else finished with your plate?"

"Don't worry about that, Kathy'll be out in a minute to collect them." Gordon took a healthy swig from his bottle of beer.

"No trouble at all." Logan collected two more plates and started for the house. Yeah, let the little woman take care of the dishes, he thought.

Kathy looked up from slicing the pie when he walked into the kitchen. "Logan."

"Came to make sure Tess wasn't in here scarfing down all the pie."

"I made three," Kathy told him with a smile.

Logan set the dishes on the kitchen counter. "Can I help?"

Tess reached for a nearby tray and began putting dishes of pie on it. "You can pass these out if you want."

They exchanged a look. Tess nodded to indicate that everything was okay.

A floral arrangement caught his eye as he waited for the tray to be filled. "Anniversary?"

Kathy shook her head. "No. Gordon sometimes just buys them for me for no reason."

"Doghouse flowers," Tess murmured, as Kathy turned around to get another pie.

Logan carried the tray out to the backyard, and Tess helped pass the plates of pie around.

Gordon was holding court still, seeming to impress some of his guests with his knowledge of the Italian statesman Machiavelli and his brilliant work called *The Prince* about how to rise to power. Then, when some of his guests looked at each other blankly, he smoothly switched to regaling them with a tale of hunting down one of the more colorful criminals of years past. With his genial smile and good ole Southern boy drawl, he was apparently quite a popular guy.

Likeable. But trying a little too hard, in Logan's opinion.

He shook off the criticism. It wasn't like him to be judgmental.

But he was glad on some level that Tess didn't seem to like Gordon, although she never showed it, and was professional and unfailingly polite around him. She looked up to him as a mentor for police work, but her nature was nothing like his.

This was the first time members of the department had gotten together since Logan arrived. It was much like the casual get-togethers back in Chicago although the accents were different. He found himself relaxing and enjoying the kind of easy camaraderie born of a mutual passion for the work and the area.

The pie was a hit, and a little while later guests began leaving. Tess stayed to help her aunt clean up, so Logan did as well. He liked the grateful look Tess gave him, but that's not why he did it. It just seemed the polite thing to do as a guest.

He was walking under one of the trees when a big brown bug unexpectedly flew at him, and he tossed the paper dishes he was carrying up into the air and yelled.

"What was that about?" Gordon asked, hurrying over.

"Biggest roach I've ever seen came out of that tree," Logan said as he bent to pick up the plates.

Tess rushed out into the back yard. "Logan? What's the matter?"

Gordon crowed. "Boy saw a palmetto bug. Screamed like a girl."

"I did not," Logan said. "Tess, I swear it was a roach that was a foot long, and it flew at me!"

He could tell she was trying to stifle a laugh. "Welcome to Florida."

"Not funny," he growled, not believing she was finding it funny.

She patted his shoulder. "Time to take you to the alligator farm and see what you think of that. You haven't seen Florida until you've seen your first alligator."

"They keep them penned up, right?" he asked as he followed her back into the house.

"Yeah, but they've got this zipline you can ride over the pen full of them."

He put the plates into a garbage bag. "What, is that supposed to be some kind of good ole boy fun or something?"

She laughed. "Tourists love it."

"Gordon likes that kind of thing," Kathy said as she rinsed some silverware under running water and stuck it in the dishwasher. "He loves putting himself in danger like that. Said he's tired of pushing paper around since he got his last promotion. But he sure works hard for those promotions and seems to enjoy playing politics to get them."

Logan thought about that. Some people really enjoyed that sort of thing.

Tess's cell rang, and she pulled it out and took the call. Logan could tell it was bad news right away. She told whoever it was she'd be right there and looked at him.

"I gotta go. Mrs. Ramsey's daughter called me. They took her mother to the hospital. Someone broke in and hurt her."

"Let's go," he said.

"You don't have to—"

He just gave her a look and crossed the room to give his hostess a hug. "Kathy, thanks for having me."

She patted his cheek. "We almost got through a whole evening without one of you being called out."

"Leave the rest of it, and I'll come back tomorrow and help out," Tess told her.

"Okay."

Tess narrowed her eyes. "You're lying to me."

Kathy grinned. "Oh, get going. There's nothing much left to do. Maybe Gordon will help. I'll bribe him with another beer. I hope Mrs. Ramsey's okay. I'll say a prayer for her."

"Me, too," said Tess as she headed out the door with Logan. "Me, too."

15

Tess walked into the emergency room waiting area and spotted Lindsey.

"How is she doing?"

"I don't know. They made me wait out here," Lindsey said, her lips trembling. "Her neighbor called me when she didn't come to the door this morning. She was unconscious when they brought her in."

She wiped the tears from her cheeks with her hands. "Why would someone hurt an old lady, Tess? She wouldn't hurt a fly."

"Let me go see what I can find out."

Tess glanced at Logan. He nodded and sat beside Lindsey, offering her a tissue from a box on a nearby table and talking quietly to her.

She spotted a familiar face and headed toward her. "How's Mrs. Ramsey?"

Susan, an R.N. Tess had gone to school with, shook her head. "It's not looking good. Dr. Langford is worried about her. She got bashed in the head pretty hard. She's having a CAT scan right now. I was just going out to talk with her daughter."

"Is she able to talk?"

"I'll have to clear it with Dr. Langford—"

"One minute. That's all I'm asking. I wouldn't ask if it wasn't so important."

Susan nodded and hurried down the hall. When she returned, she took Tess to a cubicle.

Mrs. Ramsey looked pale and shaky, but she was awake and recognized Tess. "Lindsey didn't have to call you."

Tess pulled over a chair and sat beside the gurney. "Who did this to you, Mrs. Ramsey? Did you see who hurt you?"

The woman started to shake her head, and then she moaned and held her hand to her head. "No, I woke up and someone was in the bedroom. The cats were hissing and carrying on. All I saw was this shape coming at me and then he hit me. Before I passed out, I could hear him yelping. I think one of the cats bit him or scratched him. I think it was Brutus."

She began crying. "My head hurts so bad. Is Lindsey here? Can I see Lindsey?"

Tess patted her hand. "I'll go get her. You take care and get better, okay? I'll stop back by later and see how you are."

"My cats," Mrs. Ramsey said. "I have to get out of here and take care of my cats."

"I'll stop by and see your neighbor," Tess promised her. "She has a key, right? I'm sure she'll be happy to take care of your cats until you're back home."

Tess went out to talk to Lindsey and was glad to be the bearer of good news. Lindsey sprang to her feet, ready to go back and see her mother. Tess rose and touched her arm.

"Logan and I need to go by and look over the scene," she said.

"I'll call Mom's neighbor and have her let you in," Lindsey said, pulling out her cell phone. "I'll be there right after I see Mom settled in a room."

The neighbor let Tess and Logan into the house, and then waited on the porch until they told her she could go inside.

After donning booties for their shoes and plastic gloves for their hands, Tess went straight for the bedroom while Logan checked to see where the intruder had entered.

"Logan!"

He appeared in the doorway. "Yeah?"

"Look at this." Tess waved a hand at the jewelry box on the dresser. It had been dumped and jewelry items lay in a heap. A diamond pendant and chain lay sparkling atop a pile of costume jewelry.

"The diamond necklace?"

Tess nodded. "Could be, could be a different one. But Mrs. Ramsey never said she had two and this fits the description. Oval stone, about a carat, white gold setting, and chain. We'll confirm with Lindsey."

A cat strolled in, a big white Persian Tess thought looked permanently cranky. "Brutus?"

The cat meowed and brushed up against Tess's leg. An idea began to form.

The forensics team arrived, and one of them poked his head into the room. "We found the sliding glass door forced open. Steve's taking prints now."

Tess picked up the cat and petted it. Brutus reacted with a purr. The visits to Mrs. Ramsey had paid off in a cooperative cat.

So far.

She turned to the female forensics technician on the scene. "Sally, you like cats, right?"

The woman narrowed her eyes. "Yeah. Why?"

"The victim said she thinks Brutus here scratched the perp. I'm thinking if we can get some scrapings we can check the DNA."

"We can try," Sally said. "If the cat doesn't cooperate, some-one will have to take it to a vet for the scrapings."

"Let me see if there are some treats we can bribe Brutus with first," Logan suggested.

"Good idea."

He returned with a bag of treats but Brutus just looked at them disdainfully. "What is it with cats?" he asked. "You can get a dog to do anything for a treat."

"Let's see what happens if you hold her, Tess," Sally told her. "Logan, hold this slide for me."

She gingerly reached for one of Brutus's paws and touched the claws with a Q-tip, then smeared it on the glass slide Logan held out.

Tess continued to pet the cat and talk to it reassuringly. Brutus let them swab at three feet and then objected to the fourth.

"I think that's enough," Sally said, backing away as the cat started hissing. "He probably just used the front two paws to scratch anyway."

Tess patted the cat's head and praised it before setting it down. Using a pencil, she turned back to sift through the jewelry lying on top of the dresser.

Steve poked his head in. "Daughter's here."

"I'll be right out. You can come in here next. Look for prints on the jewelry box, DNA on the bed, the works."

Tess dropped the necklace into a plastic evidence baggie. When she walked out onto the porch, she asked Lindsey if she'd heard any more about her mother's condition.

"She's got a concussion, but the doctor thinks she'll be okay. She'll be in the hospital for a few days."

"That's good to hear." She held up the baggie. "This your mom's?"

Lindsey's eyes lit up. "You found it! I thought it was gone forever! That's the one Pop gave her."

"It fits the description of the one she's claimed someone stole."

"Mom wouldn't lie," Lindsey said, frowning. "And she has her moments of confusion, early dementia. But I've looked everywhere for that necklace for her and never found it. Where was it?"

Tess exchanged a look with Logan. "In her jewelry box, right on top of costume jewelry dumped out on the dresser."

"It wasn't in her jewelry box before. I've looked so many times." Lindsey pushed at her bangs. "I don't understand. The burglar was in her room, so why didn't he take it?"

"Could be there wasn't time," Logan said. "Could be Brutus got him before he had a chance to."

"Your mom said she thought Brutus scratched the guy."

"Good ole Brutus. I'm gonna see if there's a can of tuna just for him." She looked at Tess. "Do you have to take the necklace for evidence?"

Tess shook her head. "You keep it safe at your house for now."

Lindsey sighed. "What a mystery. You get called here a dozen or more times and there's no break-in and no necklace and then there's a break in and the necklace appears? What do you make of that?"

Tess looked at Logan. "Yeah, what do you make of that?"

⸺◦⊷◦⸺

Tess clutched the steering wheel so tightly her knuckles were white. When she glanced at Logan during a stop at a red light he saw her frown.

"Let's stop and talk for a moment," he suggested quietly.

"We'll be late."

"Tess."

She sighed, checked her rear-view mirror, then signaled and pulled over on the side of the road.

"Talk to me. Tell me what's going on."

Tess rested her forehead on the steering wheel for a moment, and then she sat back. "It's just so hard having to go talk to Sam's mother. We should have caught her daughter's killer by now. I am discouraged I can't go to her with better news."

He reached for her hand, and she let him take it. "You don't handle frustration well."

"Does anyone?"

"Sure. The people who don't care enough never even get frustrated. It's not wrong to care too much. But you can't do this to yourself."

He looked out the window. While he certainly didn't want to go back to Chicago and damp, depressing fall days, it was taking some getting used to having an almost endless supply of sunny days. Even on the days it was going to rain, the TV meteorologist would label the day as "partly sunny." Huh?

"We need to work as hard as we can and keep our eyes and ears open, but it's all God's timing."

When she turned to stare at him, he shrugged, a little embarrassed. "What?"

"You don't often talk like that. I mean, I know you're a Christian but . . ." she trailed off.

"A quiet one," he said finally. "Probably not always a very good one." He took a deep breath. "Actually, I was thinking of asking if I could go with you to your church on Sunday. If you're not afraid of being with someone who'll make the place fall down."

She smiled and started up the car again. "I'm sure that won't happen. If it did, it would have the time I finally made it back after Sam died."

They rode in silence, each lost in thought. When they pulled into the driveway, Logan didn't get out immediately, preferring to let her move at her own pace.

The house was modest, a little bungalow like many on the street. The yard looked neat and well kept.

"She never moved, never changed Sam's room. It's exactly the way she left it—even to the clothes thrown on the bed that night when Sam dressed for the prom."

Tess turned to him. "Kind of like a shrine, but not. You know, it's like her mom knows she won't be coming through the door any minute, but there's that hope."

He nodded. "The person who got killed isn't the only victim. Lives stop and sometimes they don't get restarted." He stroked her cheek. "We'll go in when you're ready. Because whether it hurts or not, I know you'll make yourself do it."

She touched his hand, and her eyes were full of emotion. "I'm ready."

"And Tess? You do have something new to tell her. There's someone new on the case who's going to look at every piece of evidence there is. Not saying I'm better than you or any of the other detectives. Just maybe it'll help having someone give the case fresh look. Maybe I'll see something new."

"You're right," she said, nodding slowly. "It *is* something new. And I desperately hope you *do* find something we missed and we catch the killer before he wrecks more lives." She paused. "I'm glad you came here, Logan. For more than one reason."

She opened the door and was out of the car before he could ask her what another reason was.

He scrambled out and quickly followed her. "More than one reason?"

She shot him a quick grin. "We'll talk about it later."

Logan watched her take the stairs two at a time. She rang the doorbell, and her grin faded as a woman came to the door.

"Tess! Thanks for coming!" she said, hugging Tess and looking to Logan.

"Mrs. Marshall, this is Logan McMillan, my new partner."

She shook his hand. "Nice to meet you. Come on in."

They sat in a living room that reminded Logan of his grandmothers. Nothing had changed since the eighties with its shades of pink and mauve. Photos of Sam dominated the room.

"You made my favorite cookies!" Tess exclaimed. "You didn't have to do that."

"It was my pleasure. Logan, I hope you like butterscotch oatmeal cookies." She held out the plate to him.

He reached for one and bit in. "Never had one. This is good."

She poured coffee for them, and Logan sat back and let Tess control the pace of the time with Mrs. Marshall. His eyes swept the room. He saw evidence of a loving relationship between mother and daughter in the photos displayed around the room. He remembered what Tess had said about Sam's mother not changing anything about Sam's room.

He looked at Tess, and she caught his silent message.

"Mrs. Marshall, I asked you if you'd talk with us today for a reason."

"Yes?"

"I wanted to introduce you to Logan. He's helping us take a fresh new look at Sam's murder. I'm hoping he's going to find something we missed."

The woman looked at Logan with such hope his heart ached. "Tess and the rest of the police department have worked so hard, I don't know how they could have missed anything. But I'm hoping you find her killer, Logan. I'm praying for it."

Tess reached over and squeezed her hand. "We are, too."

"Tess tells me you've kept everything as it was before Sam was killed. Would you mind if I looked at her bedroom?"

"Of course. It's the second door on the left."

He went into the room painted a pale shade of pink. A proud mother had framed and hung awards on the walls—Honor Society, citizenship, the local humane society student volunteer of the year. She'd been a busy girl and a popular one from the photos of friends displayed on the top of her dresser.

Logan bent and looked at each of them. There were many shots of Tess and Sam—happy ones of them from elementary school up to high school. He felt his heart aching for a second time as he studied Tess's face. There was innocence, joy, a hopefulness, and he couldn't help mourning the loss of them.

Focused on the emotion, his throat tightening, he started to turn away and then he found himself turning to stare at the photo of Sam taken at a prom. He recognized her dress from photos of her lying dead in it and realized it was her senior prom photo. This one was a professional photo, and in it she stood with Wendell.

"Logan?"

"Hmm?" He looked up, distracted.

"Everything okay?"

"Come look at this photo," he said, holding it out to her.

She took it and studied it. "I've never seen this one."

"Oh, the prom photographer sent that a couple of weeks after Sam was killed," Mrs. Marshall said as she came into the room. "I put the photo away and only got it out to frame it months later."

"Tess, look at what's around her neck," Logan said.

She looked and then stared at him, her eyes wide. "It's Mrs. Ramsey's necklace."

16

Tess turned to Mrs. Marshall. "We have to go. Thank you for the cookies."

"Let me pack some up for you—"

"Sorry, no time!" She grabbed her purse and jogged out the door.

"Nice to meet you, Mrs. Marshall!" Logan called over his shoulder.

"Nice to meet you, too! Come back sometime when you have more time!"

The minute they were in the car, Tess threw it into gear and sped out of the driveway. "Call it in—"

Logan already had his cell phone out and was calling the hospital to ask that security go to Mrs. Ramsey's room until he got an officer there.

"We have to get the results from the cat's claws," he muttered when he finished his call to the station. "The killer was right in her room. Bet Brutus gets treated to a can of tuna after we tell Mrs. Ramsey he saved her life."

"Doesn't fit the profile," Tess said, keeping her eye on the road. She slowed, then stopped behind other cars as the drawbridge went up on the Bridge of Lions. She pounded her fist on the steering wheel.

Logan's cell rang. He answered it, listened, thanked the caller, and then hung up. "We've got Mrs. Ramsey covered. Gordon was there."

"At the hospital?"

"Yeah. There, drawbridge is going down." He turned to her. "Your aunt is in the ER. She had a fall. Again."

Tess glanced at him. "Why do you say 'again'?"

"I think Gordon's abusing her."

A car horn sounded. Tess waved her hand and continued across the bridge. "I suspected the same thing the last time she fell, but she insisted she tripped over the cat."

"What do *you* think?"

Tess sighed. "I kept blaming the fact I don't like Gordon for my suspicions."

Logan drummed his fingers on his knee. "There's usually a reason we don't like someone."

"It's not anything I can really put my finger on," she said slowly. "I just feel uncomfortable around him. I can usually tell he's near before I see him. Part of that is because he likes to pop up and startle people. Drives Aunt Kathy crazy."

She frowned. "I remember her starting to chide him for that at the hospital last time she was in. Then there's this thing . . ."

"Yeah?"

"Well, have you ever watched *The Andy Griffith Show*? I know it was a little before our time, but it's in reruns on some stations."

"I'm familiar with it," he said dryly. "It's part of the culture."

"Gordon reminds me of affable Andy everyone loves. We call them good ole boys here in the South. I'm not saying Andy or good ole boys are bad. But I just sense something . . . darker about Gordon. It's just he seems so likable and good-natured on the surface, but then he's not been so nice to my aunt for some time."

When she stopped at a light, she turned to him. "He seems very ambitious, too, but not in a good way. I gather he's really looking to the time when the chief steps down." She pushed at her bangs. "Then there's the way he talked about the homeless the day we questioned the man we brought in."

"I remember."

"I hope my aunt's okay."

"We're almost there. You go check on her, and I'll talk to Mrs. Ramsey. Come up to her room when you can."

Tess pulled into a parking spot reserved for police and got out. "See you."

Logan stopped her with a hand on her arm. "I'll say a prayer for your aunt. Call me if you need me."

He kissed her cheek and strode off, leaving her to stare at his retreating back.

"Wow," she muttered and then walked into the emergency room.

She identified herself at the desk and was shown to the cubicle where her aunt lay pale and still on a gurney.

The nurse attending her held her finger to her lips. "We sedated her. She's about to go upstairs for surgery. Broken jaw."

She nodded and touched her aunt's hand. "I want to stay with her until she goes upstairs."

"That's fine. I'll tell the doctor you're here."

Tess sank into the chair next to the gurney and waited.

When the doctor came in a few minutes later, he was frowning. "I thought her husband was going to stay with her until she went to surgery."

"Police emergency. He'll be back when he's relieved in a few minutes. I was told my aunt was here, but not how she got injured."

He hesitated, glanced at his patient, and then met her gaze. "She said she fell."

"And broke her jaw?"

"Yeah. It could happen."

"But did it." Tess didn't phrase it as a question. "I'm not just her niece. I'm a cop. If it's domestic abuse, I need to look into it."

"I was just checking her records. She's been in here several times in the past year. If it's not domestic abuse, then she needs a good evaluation to find out why she's so accident-prone."

He pushed up wire-rimmed glasses that had slipped down his nose. "I'm sure you don't need to be told that cops have a high rate of domestic abuse."

A statement not a question.

The curtain closing off the cubicle snapped open, revealing Gordon "Hey, Tess, Logan said you were here. How's Kathy?"

"About to go up to surgery," the doctor told him. "You can wait upstairs in the surgical waiting room." With a nod, he left them.

Tess stood. "I'll be up in a minute. I want to check in with Logan first."

"I hope now that Mrs. Ramsey has found her necklace, she'll stop calling 911."

"Gordon, someone tried to hurt her last night. We think it was the serial killer."

"Nah, she's just a crazy old bat."

"She isn't a crazy old bat. She just hasn't been the same since—"

"Yeah, yeah, since your friend Samantha died."

"I'll see you in the waiting room after I talk to Logan." She left and made her way upstairs to Mrs. Ramsey's room.

"How's your aunt?" Logan asked the moment Tess walked up to him outside Mrs. Ramsey's room.

"She's in surgery. Broken jaw."

He raised his brows. "And?"

Tess took a deep breath. "I'm talking with her as soon as she's out of surgery. Have you spoken to Mrs. Ramsey yet?"

"I waited for you."

"Let's do it." She knocked at the door and heard Lindsey, Mrs. Ramsey's daughter, call for them to enter.

"Why, Tess, Logan! What a nice surprise!"

Tess bent to kiss Mrs. Ramsey on the cheek. "We need to talk to you some more about what happened the other night."

"Sure." She patted a place on the bed. "Sit here and Logan, grab a chair over there. No one's in the other bed."

Logan caught the look of strain around Tess's eyes and mouth. Silently he asked if she wanted him to take the lead, and she nodded.

"Mrs. Ramsey, we want to talk to you about your necklace."

She sat up straighter in her bed. "I didn't misplace that necklace. I don't know why it was suddenly in the jewelry box that night."

"We know, Mrs. Ramsey," Logan said quietly.

"Well, I can't think why someone would break in and put it back," she said, looking confused.

"We can. It's not going to be pleasant what we have to tell you, but I know you want the truth."

She nodded.

"Mrs. Ramsey, the necklace disappeared the night of the prom," Tess said, picking up where Logan had left off. "I think you forgot you gave it or loaned it to Sam that night, and after she was found you were so upset you forgot about it."

Realization dawned in Mrs. Ramsey's eyes. "Yes, I did. She was feeling a little down because she was in a borrowed dress and all."

"Well, the killer took the necklace that night, Mrs. Ramsey. Sometimes these kinds of killers do that. They take an object from the victim. It's like taking a trophy if that makes any sense."

She nodded. "I've heard that. But why did he bring it back?"

Then a look of horror washed over her face. "Oh—oh, my, Logan, are you saying the man who broke into my house and left the necklace was the man who killed Sam?"

Logan glanced at Tess and then at Mrs. Ramsey. "Yes," he said. "That's what we're saying."

Lindsey made a strangled sound.

"You okay?" Tess asked her. "Let me get you some water." She poured a plastic glass full from a small pitcher on Mrs. Ramsey's bedside table.

"Thanks," Lindsey said after she took a sip. "I'll be okay."

"We've had security on your room since we came to this conclusion a little while ago," Tess told her. "And we'll have someone here and at your house until we find the killer."

"You're coming home with me," Lindsey said firmly.

"Then we'll have an officer parked outside there." Logan leaned forward. "Mrs. Ramsey, Tess and I have been talking about the necklace, wondering why anyone would return it."

"Well it's obvious, isn't it?" Mrs. Ramsey said tartly. "I just look like a crazy old lady, don't I?"

Logan saw Tess tense. They exchanged a look, and she shook her head slightly.

"Why would someone care if she looks like a crazy old lady?" Lindsey asked, puzzled.

"Maybe he thinks she knows something." Logan mused.

The three women stared at him.

"But I don't know anything," Mrs. Ramsey insisted.

"Mama, maybe you know something, but you don't know you know it," Lindsey suggested.

"Well, that's just crazy."

"No, it isn't," Logan said and he sprang to his feet and paced around the room. "We'll start with the day of the prom and work through it until the time Sam went missing."

"If you feel up to it," Tess said. "We'll take it in steps. You let us know when we need to stop and let you rest, okay?"

Mrs. Ramsey folded her arms across her chest. "I'm ready, and I'm not going to need a rest. I want this creep caught."

There was a knock on the door.

"Come in!" Lindsey called.

Gordon stuck his head in. His eyes swept the room until he saw Tess. "Just thought I'd let you know Kathy's out of surgery."

"Thanks, I'll come down in a few minutes."

He nodded and closed the door.

"Your aunt is here having surgery?" Mrs. Ramsey asked. "Oh my dear, you should be with her, not here with me."

"She'd be upset with me if I did that instead of doing my job," Tess assured her.

"At least go check on her, and I'll talk to Logan."

"Go," Logan told her. "It'll just take a few minutes."

Tess left the room. Logan turned to Mrs. Ramsey and opened his notebook. "So tell me about prom night."

She began telling him about how she'd volunteered to be a chaperone that night. "Two of my favorite students were graduating, and it was their senior prom," she said. "Oh, I know we're not supposed to have favorites, but Tess and Sam were two of my brightest and hardest-working students. And Tess became a sort of daughter to me after her mother died earlier that year."

"I didn't mind," Lindsey said. "Losing her mom was so hard on Tess."

"The girls decorated the venue for the prom," Mrs. Ramsey continued, her eyes taking on a faraway expression as she remembered. "Then they went to change, and they were so pretty. It was when Sam said something to me about she felt like Second Hand Rose in her borrowed gown and a rhinestone necklace that I took off the necklace my husband had given me for our anniversary and put it around her neck myself."

She glanced at Lindsey. "I knew it was safe with her. After all, I was right there during the dance. And even if it was valuable, well, we had security for the prom. You know, to keep problems away, the students maybe doing the usual like sneaking booze into the punch or having a fistfight and such."

Logan remembered his own prom. "When did you notice Sam missing?"

"I saw her slip out with her date. You know, Wendell, he became an attorney. Some of the couples would do that, and we chaperones would just send one of the security we'd hired to round them up in the parking lot and send them back inside."

"Not that security was so good," she said, frowning. "That Gordon must have shaped up some to have gotten as high in your department as he has. We needed him a couple of times that night and couldn't find him."

"Mother!" Lindsey spoke up. "Don't go badmouthing him again. It's enough that you said that to his face a couple of weeks ago when we ran into him at church, isn't it?"

"I'm sorry," Mrs. Ramsey rushed to say.

"It's the dementia," Lindsey said quietly. "She remembers stuff from the past so vividly."

Mrs. Ramsey frowned in concentration. "Anyway, I remember Sam wasn't the only one who went outside with Wendell that night. He ended up marrying the other girl not long after they graduated. Her name's Muffi."

She paused and looked thoughtful. "But after Wendell and Sam went out he came back in and she didn't." She looked at Logan. "She never came back in. The police talked to him later, but they said he wasn't a suspect."

Logan remembered his interview with the man. He wanted him to be a suspect, but he and Tess had had to take him off the list. Muffi had given him an alibi, and they hadn't been able to poke any holes in it.

Mrs. Ramsey looked like she was tiring, but when he asked if she needed a break she refused. Lindsey stood and poured her mother a glass of water. Mrs. Ramsey sipped it and answered more questions about how Tess had become concerned about her friend and they'd gone looking for her. Tears slipped down Mrs. Ramsey's cheeks as she described the horror of them checking the park and finding Sam's body.

Lindsey handed her mother a tissue. Mrs. Ramsey dabbed at her cheeks. "I'm so glad Tess isn't here to relive that night."

Logan didn't have the heart to tell her he doubted that night was ever very far from Tess's memory.

By the time Tess returned, Logan felt he'd gotten everything he could from Mrs. Ramsey. He was ready to leave when she walked in.

"How's your aunt?" he asked her.

"Resting comfortably," she said. "They don't expect her to wake tonight, so I'm going to come back in the morning. Gordon's staying for a while."

Logan watched her give her former teacher a hug, and they left. An officer stood outside and nodded to them as they left.

"We need to stop on the third floor," she said when they entered the elevator. "Chief's been admitted for tests."

"Really? I know he's been feeling under the weather."

They checked at the third floor nurse's station, got the room number, and went to pay a visit.

He looked up in surprise as they entered his room. "Hey, didn't know anyone knew I was here."

"Gordon's downstairs with Kathy," Tess told him. "She fell and had to have surgery. I sat with her while Gordon took care of an emergency."

"Kathy had surgery? She seemed okay when she was here visiting me with him." He frowned. "Gordon didn't say anything."

The chief gestured at the empty plastic container on his bedside table. "He and Kathy visited me earlier today. She brought me some chicken soup since I was complaining about the hospital food."

They chatted for a few minutes. Well, Logan and the chief chatted with Logan filling him in on the latest development with Mrs. Ramsey's interview. Tess seemed quiet. Logan figured she was worried about her aunt.

The chief's wife walked in then with coffee she'd evidently bought from the cafeteria downstairs. Logan and Tess excused themselves, and they were nearly out the door when Tess suddenly spun around and walked back into the room.

"If you don't mind, I'll take this and drop it at my aunt's house on my way home," she told the chief. She looked at his wife. "You know how some women are about their Tupperware being returned."

The woman rolled her eyes. "Do I ever! Lucy Vanderwell gave me such grief about leaving hers in the church kitchen after a women's luncheon. Give your aunt my best, okay?"

"Will do."

"Why didn't you say something?" Logan asked as they got into the elevator. "You started to say something about suspecting Gordon of abusing your aunt, didn't you?"

Tess nodded.

"So why didn't you?"

"He and the chief are friends. And the chief's his boss. I have to be very careful to have proof before I say anything."

Logan sighed. "You did the right thing. Talk to your aunt, and you'll know what to do."

17

Nice service."

Tess smiled at Logan as they stood. "Told you that you'd like it here."

Logan glanced around as they walked to the front of the church. "And the walls stayed up."

"Yeah. Imagine that."

"Tess! So nice to see you!"

"This is Logan McMillan," she introduced him. "Logan's my partner. He's a detective who's transferred from Chicago. Logan, Pastor Rick "

The two men shook hands. "Pleasure to meet you. Guess you're not going to miss those cold winters."

"Probably not. Although I sure miss the pizza."

"Tess, take him by Angelo's. Bet he can make a deep-dish."

"I'll do that."

"Hope you'll join us again, Logan. Any friend of Tess's is a friend of ours."

"And what am I, chopped liver?" a familiar voice boomed.

Tess tried not to stiffen. She turned. "Gordon. I didn't expect you here this morning. How's Aunt Kathy?"

"Just fine, just fine." He turned to the pastor. "Kathy took a spill," he explained as he shook hands with him. "Had surgery and should be going home tomorrow."

Tess and Logan walked outside. Gordon followed them. "Listen, do you think you could drop by and check on her now, Tess? Chief asked me to take care of some things in his absence."

"How's he doing?" Logan asked.

"Just great. They're running some tests to figure out why his stomach's been giving him fits. I think it's stress. 'Bout time he retired."

Tess had intended to see her aunt after she had lunch with Logan, but when she glanced at him, he nodded. "Of course. How about I stop at your house and pick up a few things to make her more comfortable at the hospital? Maybe one of her nightgowns and a robe?"

"Sure thing. You still got your key?"

"Yes. Do you need me to feed the cat?"

He shook his head. "I put kibble down for her before I left for church." He glanced down at his hand and showed them bright red scratches. "That's the thanks I got for doing it. Dang cat. I'd boot her out of the house if Kathy wouldn't give me a fit."

He looked up as someone called his name. "There's Tom Crandall. I need to talk with him. He's going to do some renovations on Kathy's shop. See you both later."

Tess glanced at Logan. "Sorry, I know we talked about having lunch after church."

"I don't mind tagging along on the visit, if you don't. I like your aunt. Then we could have lunch afterward."

"It can't exactly be fun to go visit someone in the hospital on your day off."

"Being with you is fun. Doesn't matter what we do."

Her heart warmed. "Ditto."

She'd picked him up in her car for church so they walked to it. As Tess got in she saw Gordon watching them as he stood talking with another man on the church steps. Frowning, she fastened her seat belt and waited until Logan did so before she pulled out of the lot.

"What?"

She shrugged. "I intended on going to see Aunt Kathy later today, but I think Gordon should be checking on her before he takes care of anything for the chief. After all, she's his wife."

"Won't get any argument from me about that."

Tess pulled into her aunt's driveway. "I'll be right back."

She let herself into the house and Prissy looked up from the sofa and blinked. "Hi there. Just getting some things for your mom. She'll be home tomorrow."

Good thing Logan waited in the car, she couldn't help thinking. He'd probably think she was nutty to talk to Aunt Kathy's cat that way.

It was quick work to pack an overnight bag with the essentials she knew her aunt would want: a makeup kit, a nightgown and robe. And the quilt she'd taken last time—the blue memory one her aunt had made for her mother-in-law so many years ago. It had seemed to comfort Aunt Kathy when she took it to the hospital on the last visit.

This was going to be the last hospital visit if she had anything to say about it. The first chance she got to talk to Aunt Kathy, she was going to get her to come live with her until they figured out what to do. She hoped she could get her aunt to talk to Pastor Rick, get some professional counseling. Abusers seldom changed. Divorce—as much as Tess hated the idea—seemed the only answer.

It wasn't her place to tell her aunt or God what to do. But something had to be done.

Logan was listening to the radio, his head resting on the back of the seat, his eyes closed.

"Hey, Sleeping Beauty, having a nice nap there?" she asked as she put the overnight bag in the back seat.

"Not asleep," he said in a sleepy voice. "Just resting my eyes."

"Yeah, right."

An afternoon nap seemed to be the popular thing. Aunt Kathy was taking one when they walked in. Or perhaps it was because she was still recovering from the anesthesia from the night before.

She looked peaceful . . . so peaceful. Tess set the overnight bag down on the floor beside the bed and drew out the quilt. She spread it over her aunt and gently tucked it around her shoulders.

Tess watched her aunt stir, then her eyes fluttered open. She focused on Tess. She saw the recognition in her aunt's eyes, saw the corners of her mouth try to lift in a smile and Tess could see the metal wiring inside.

Then her aunt's gaze fell on the quilt, her eyes went wide with fear and a horrible strangled sound came from between her wired jaws.

Logan watched Tess try to hold her aunt down and calm her, but it didn't seem to be doing any good.

He joined her at the bedside and pressed the call button to summon a nurse. Then he got out of the way, so she and Tess could talk to Kathy.

"I'm going to contact the doctor and see if he'll order a sedative," the nurse said and hurried out of the room.

Tess pulled up a chair and sat beside her aunt, holding her hand and stroking it while she murmured to her.

The nurse returned with the shot and Logan left the room. Tess emerged a few minutes later, looking drained.

"The nurse said Aunt Kathy would probably sleep for a couple of hours."

"Do you want to stay, and I'll go get you something to eat?"

"That's really sweet, but no. I think I'd like to get out of here for a while. I need to think."

He put his arm around her and led her down the hall to the elevator. "You think too much. Try to turn that brain off for a few hours and let's just relax."

"It was just so weird," she said on the ride down. "She woke up and looked happy to see me. Then she looked scared to death. Logan, she looked scared to death. And she tried to kick off the quilt. That's her favorite. Why would she do that?"

"I don't know." Logan had glanced at the doorway when Kathy began reacting hysterically in case she'd seen someone she was afraid of—like her husband. But no one had been standing in the doorway.

"I don't get it," Tess said, shaking her head as they walked out of the hospital.

"You're upset," he said. "Let me drive."

She handed him the keys and got into the passenger side. When she didn't ask where they were going once he started the car, he knew how upset she was. Tess always loved talking about where they were going to eat.

He drove them to a little dive she'd shown him outside of town. She claimed the fried shrimp was the best she'd ever eaten, and he'd had to agree with her. They sat outside on the deck overlooking a small pond the owner had stocked with ducks.

Gradually, she relaxed as they shared some smoked mullet spread on crackers—a local favorite she'd claimed belied the unglamorous name of the fish—and drank large glasses of sweet tea mixed with lemonade. The shrimp were perfect, golden brown and crispy, served with cole slaw and French fries. They ate until they were stuffed.

Logan wanted the mood to stay relaxed, but had to ask a question that had been bothering him. He reached across the table and took her hand, lacing her fingers with his. Again, she didn't try to avoid his touch. So far so good.

"Are we okay?" he asked quietly.

She stared at him, puzzled. "I don't know what you mean."

"Where do you see us going?"

"Going?"

He grinned at her. "I'm crazy about you, you know that?"

She eyed him warily. "I think you're just crazy."

Logan laughed and squeezed her fingers. "You know I'm not. I've never been saner."

"We haven't known each other that long. We don't know that much about each other."

He just looked at her. "I know everything I need to know. But if you need more time . . ."

Tess pushed her bangs back. "I can't even think right now. So much is going on. How can you think about stuff like this?"

Logan reached across for her other hand, and after a moment, she put hers in it. "My friend said, 'Life is too serious. Lighten up.' His death, Sam's, well, I think they should be a lesson to us to live life now, don't you?"

"Oh, it's easy to say," she said with a big sigh. "Not so easy to do."

The server came to clear the table and tempt them with dessert. Logan had tasted their Key lime pie and wasn't leaving without a slice. Besides, he knew once it arrived, Tess and her sweet tooth wouldn't be able to resist sharing it.

A few minutes later, she put her fork down and pushed back from the table. "Why couldn't you be selfish and refuse to share?"

He laughed and got to his feet. "C'mon, let's go for a walk on the beach."

Her cell rang as they got into the car. She took the call and from her answers, he could tell that it was about her aunt.

"Need to go back?"

She hesitated and then nodded. "In a while."

"Tess, we need to talk about your aunt."

She stared out the window for a long time and then when she looked back at him, she nodded. "I know. I'm going to have the talk with her as soon as she's released."

"I don't think she should go back to her house."

"I know. But I don't think she'll listen to me."

"Then who will she listen to?"

She bit her lip. "Maybe I should talk to Pastor Rick."

"Good idea. And a domestic abuse counselor? You must know some."

"I do." She thought for a moment. "I don't think Lori would mind a call, even though it's Sunday."

"Domestic abuse doesn't take a day off. Bet if you know someone who works in it, she won't mind a phone call."

Tess pulled out her cell and texted a message. "Let's take that walk. Or are you ready for a nap, Yankee?"

He laughed. "As I recall, I won our last race."

"I let you," she told him smugly. "I ran track in college. I felt sorry for you that day, because it was so hot and you hadn't adjusted to the temperature and humidity. "

"You ran track, huh? I didn't know that," he said as he started the car. "I did, too."

"See, I told you we didn't know enough about each other."

He shot her a quelling look. "I hardly think I need to know you ran track before we walk down the aisle."

Her eyes went wide, and she paled. Logan found himself holding his breath as he waited for her reaction.

"Married?"

He might not have meant it to come out the way it had, but she didn't need to look so surprised. "Where'd you think I was headed?"

"I—I don't know."

Logan needed to move, needed to do something. He ran his hands over the steering wheel, started the car, and pulled out of the lot.

"The thing is, I'm not a casual kind of person and you're not either," he told her as he headed for her house. "So I guess if you're not interested in that being in our future, you should let me know."

"Just like that?" she demanded as she snapped on her seat belt. "You can't just dump something like that in my lap and expect an instant response."

"I'm not asking for a yes or no right now—"

"Good thing, because it wouldn't be fair!"

He glanced at her when they had to stop for a light. "You had to know this was coming."

"Are you calling me dense?" Her eyes flashed.

Oops. Logan had been around enough years to recognize that tone. Watch it, he told himself.

"Of course not," he said carefully. "Just a little slow?"

"I'll show you slow," she muttered when she got out of the car. "I'll be right back."

She might have been slow on noticing the signals he was becoming seriously interested in her, but the woman was back in a flash and dressed in running gear.

"I'll be just a minute," he told her when he pulled into his driveway. "You can come in if you want."

"I'll stay here." She folded her arms across her chest and looked out the window.

"Okay. I thought you might want to meet Joe. We don't get much company."

"Oh, all right."

She followed him into the house and glanced around. "I don't see any cat. I suppose next you'll want me to see your etchings?"

"Sorry, haven't unpacked them yet," he said easily.

She walked over to an open box. "When were you intending to unpack?"

"Been working too many hours." He pulled off his tie. "And besides, I kept thinking I'd be buying a house. It'd just be easier not to have to pack everything up again."

She looked up at him and nodded. "Makes sense. But it doesn't help to make you feel at home right now, does it?"

He shrugged. "I hang out with this woman who makes me feel at home when I'm around her."

"Don't go saying things like that. It's not fair."

"Who said I was fair?"

Joe came out of the bedroom, and when he saw Tess he strolled over to check her out. Logan watched Tess bend to pet him.

"Aren't you a handsome fellow?" she asked him, and he preened, lifting his head and rubbing it against her hand.

Handsome? Logan rolled his eyes. Joe looked like the tough alley cat he'd been before Logan had taken him on. He had a chunk missing out of one ear and a big patch of fur still growing back where the vet had stitched an open wound from a fight the first time Logan took him in.

"I'll just leave the two of you to get acquainted."

Tess walked over, sat on the sofa, and patted the cushion beside her. Joe ran to join her and settled, purring, beside her.

"He's never come once for me when I called him," Logan muttered as he headed for the bedroom. "Traitor."

While he was changing, he took a call about a case he was investigating. By the time he returned to the living room, nearly twenty minutes had passed. He found Tess dozing on the sofa, the cat tucked beneath her arm.

Joe opened one eye and stared at him.

"Stealing my girl, eh?"

The cat just blinked and closed his eyes again.

Logan debated waking Tess and decided against it for a few minutes. He sat in a nearby armchair and watched her. Felt . . . right to have her in his space.

He hadn't really been honest with her, though—he'd never gotten around to looking for a house since they'd been seeing each other. He wasn't quite at the point of thinking where they'd live if they got married, but he liked her little house a lot. It felt like home to him.

"So why didn't you wake me?"

Logan opened his eyes and focused on Tess lying on his sofa. "Are you admitting you fell asleep?"

"Yeah." She glanced down at the cat that slept on. "Once he did I think I just drifted off. Great nap sofa."

He yawned and checked his watch. "Probably half the people who went to church are taking naps right now. Sacred Sunday tradition."

"It isn't just because it's Sunday," she said. "Both of us have been working too much overtime. I can't remember the last time I got enough sleep. And forget about exercise. I haven't been running in ages."

She sat up and moved the cat. Joe shifted and didn't open an eye. "What time is it?"

"A little after three."

"I'm going to go visit Aunt Kathy."

"After we take that run you mentioned."

She lifted her chin. "Yeah. After we run, and I beat you."

"You mean after you try. It's a nice cool day, and I'm acclimated to the weather now, even if I wasn't the last time. You won't have the advantage today."

Logan got to his feet and stretched.

"Big talk," she scoffed and stood. "We'll see, won't we?"

He headed for the kitchen. "I'll get some bottled water. You say goodbye to Romeo there."

"Hey, don't call him that. I like him."

She was checking her cell phone for messages when he returned. "Lori says she'll be happy to talk to me this evening. She's at the playground with her kids right now."

"Good." He hesitated, then he put the bottles of water on the coffee table, sat down and patted the cushion beside him as she'd done with the cat. "Can we talk for a minute? Not about what we were discussing earlier."

She gave him a wary look, but she joined him on the sofa. Once again, he reached for her hand, and when she let him take it without reservation, he felt a little relieved.

"I've been worried about touching you," he said at last. "I was afraid that you might be nervous, since your uncle thinks it's okay to rough up a woman."

"I didn't like you calling me dense earlier—" she stopped. "Okay, so you didn't," she said quickly when he tried to correct her. "But I was slow to see what he was doing, and I feel badly about it."

He kissed her hand. "Well, I'm glad you're not flinching and you feel comfortable around me."

"I do," she said and she rose. "But I think it'd be best if we got out of here, don't you?"

"I think I remember what box I put those etchings in," he said, as he got up.

"Get the water, Romeo," she told him as she started for the door. "Bye, Joe. Hope to see you again soon."

18

Tess stopped by the hospital again the next afternoon. She frowned when she saw how pale her aunt looked. "We need to talk."

Aunt Kathy mimed that she couldn't because of her wired mouth.

"Then I'll talk," Tess said easily. She pulled a chair up beside the bed and set her tote bag on the floor. "It's past time to do something, Aunt Kathy. Before it gets out of hand and you get hurt even worse than this."

Her aunt turned her head toward the wall.

"I should have seen the signs," Tess told her. "I'm so sorry I didn't."

She watched her aunt as she continued to look away. Lori had told her that her aunt might be resistant—even deny the abuse. But she had to keep trying to get her aunt to get away and get counseling. Abusers seldom stopped. Lori had been worried, too, that a man in Gordon's position might be able to shield himself from a restraining order or prosecution.

Finally, her aunt turned back, and Tess saw the tears in her eyes. She struggled to say something Tess didn't understand and waved her hands helplessly.

Tess reached into her jacket pocket and pulled out her notepad. She offered it along with a pen, and the older woman scribbled something and held it out to her.

"Not your fault. You asked me."

She leaned forward. "I want you to press charges."

Aunt Kathy shook her head and looked frightened.

"I'll protect you," she assured her. "You can come live with me, and we'll get a restraining order."

Once again, the woman scribbled furiously. "Can't cause problems for you."

"I'm a big girl, Aunt Kathy. I can take care of myself. And you. He can't do this to you and get away with it."

The woman's agitation grew. Tess reached for her hand and squeezed it. "I spoke with a friend of mine. She's a domestic abuse counselor. I want you to talk to her."

Once again, her aunt turned her back on her.

"Hey, how's my girl?" a familiar voice boomed.

Tess watched her aunt's body tense, and then, she didn't believe her eyes as her aunt turned slowly and managed a tremulous smile for him.

All the while, she was surreptitiously tucking the notepad and pen under the covers.

Gordon acknowledged Tess with a nod as he strolled to his wife's bed and leaned down to pat her shoulder. He handed her the bunch of flowers in his hand.

"Talked to the doc, Kathy," Gordon said as he pulled a chair over to the opposite side of the bed from Tess. "He's got you scheduled for some tests to see why you lost your balance and fell."

Tess couldn't stand to sit here and listen to this. She stood and reached for the flowers. "Let me go get something to put those in."

Kathy handed them to her and smiled. Her smile faded, when she apparently realized that Tess was staring at her mouth.

A nurse found a vase Tess took back to the room. Gordon was still there, but he was getting to his feet and saying he had to go check in with the chief.

"Don't know if you've heard the chief is going to be here for a couple days," he told Tess. "He had a mild heart attack."

"Oh, no, that's awful," she said, shocked. "No, I hadn't heard. I thought he was just here for tests."

"Lucky for him he was." Gordon checked his appearance in a mirror by the door. "When he popped the heart attack he was in the right place."

He glanced at Kathy. "So I've been made acting chief. I might not be back here today, but I'll check with your doc about picking you up tomorrow."

"Do you mind if I take a few hours personal time to stay with Aunt Kathy?" Tess asked as casually as she could manage.

Gordon shrugged. "Sure. Call your supervisor and tell him I okayed it."

Tess watched him leave, then turned to her aunt. The woman was staring after her husband with big tears rolling down her face. When she saw Tess looking at her, she gestured for the flowers. Tess handed them to her and was shocked when her aunt threw them at the wastepaper basket a few feet away. Then Kathy pulled out the notepad and pen and scrawled, "No more doghouse flowers!"

"Use that anger, Aunt Kathy!" Tess said urgently. "Use it to make you leave him."

Kathy wrote on the pad and thrust it at Tess. "You don't understand!"

191

Tess picked up the flowers, put them into the wastepaper basket, and then sank down into her chair. "No, I don't. I just don't. You can't let yourself be a punching bag."

She watched Kathy press her hand to her heart, miming she loved him, and the tears started again. Tess reached over for the box of tissues on the nightstand and placed it on the bed. Then she took her aunt's hand, held it, and let her cry it out.

A nurse came in a few minutes later with a computer on a rolling cart. She checked Kathy's vital signs. "How's the pain? On a scale of one to ten?"

Kathy held up seven fingers.

"I'll get you something." She made some entries on her computer screen, then wheeled it out of the room.

"Is there anything I can get you?" When her aunt shook her head, then winced from the pain the movement caused, Tess settled back in her chair.

"You don't have to stay," Kathy wrote on the pad.

"Sorry, you're stuck with me," Tess said cheerfully.

She drew a quilt square from her tote bag. She smiled when she saw her aunt's curiosity. "These are for the lighthouse quilt. I'm putting different scenes of sights around St. Augustine as a border around its lighthouse."

This one was a sailboat riding the crest of waves, something they both often saw on the water around the Old Fort.

"A ship in a harbor is safe but that is not what a ship is built for . . ." Tess finished cross stitching the last few letters of the last word. She placed it in her aunt's hands and waited for her reaction.

She held her thumb and forefinger a tiny distance apart, and Tess nodded. "I'm trying to make my stitches smaller just like you said." Kathy nodded and did a thumbs-up.

Tess pulled out another square. This was the last one she had to do some small finishing work on before attaching it to the quilt. She stroked the shiny piece of satin cut in the shape of a ball gown to be sewn on the figure of a young woman. The figure stood beneath the swaying gray strands of Spanish moss hanging from a tree branch near the St. Augustine lighthouse.

Tess glanced up. "It's Sam. She looked so pretty in her blue prom dress, didn't she?"

She pinned the dress on and reached into her bag for the piece of blue satin fabric cut for a tiny shawl that matched the one Sam had worn that night.

"Blue," Tess said. "I wonder why the killer was obsessed with blue." She looked up at her aunt. "He always takes a piece of blue clothing or blue jewelry from the victims."

Her aunt made a noise, and Tess looked at her. Goosebumps were dancing across her arms, bare beneath the short-sleeved hospital gown.

"Oh, sweetheart, are you cold?" Tess reached over and started to draw the quilt that lay across the foot of the bed.

A cold hand clamped on hers. Startled, Tess dropped the quilt and looked at her aunt. The woman was staring at the quilt.

"I brought it yesterday," Tess told her. "I thought it might make you feel better to have something from home to keep you warm. Hospitals can be chilly."

"Gordon's mother's favorite color was blue," Kathy wrote on the notepad. "Wore it lots. Dressed her kids in it."

Then Tess felt goose bumps dance across her own skin. All of the simple squares on the quilt were blue.

It had to be a coincidence . . .

Her aunt whimpered. When Tess glanced at her, she saw her rubbing at her temples. Immediately, she felt guilty at not noticing how much pain she was in.

BARBARA CAMERON

"I wonder what's taking the nurse so long to bring in your pain meds," Tess said. "I'll go find out." She put the square on her aunt's bed and went in search of the nurse.

When she returned, Kathy was sitting in her bed clutching the square and staring at it. She looked up at Tess with frightened eyes.

"What is it?" Tess asked, rushing to her side. "I didn't mean to upset you talking about Sam."

Kathy shook her head, set the square down and pulled out the notepad. She scribbled furiously and then shoved it into Tess's hands.

"Call Logan. Get him here. Don't tell Gordon!"

———

Logan knocked on the door of Kathy's hospital room and frowned when he saw the lines of strain around Tess's mouth when she let him into the room.

"What's up?"

She glanced up and down the hall before she closed the door and gestured at him to sit.

"I was sitting here working on the lighthouse quilt," Tess said. "I was working on the square with Sam in her blue prom dress and telling Aunt Kathy that the killer favored blue clothing and jewelry. And I don't know, Logan, this might be crazy, but when I happened to put it down to pull the quilt up over Aunt Kathy, I suddenly realized . . . Logan, it's probably a coincidence her quilt is made of all blue pieces."

"Yeah," he said slowly, frowning. "I don't see where you're going with this."

"She made it out of blue clothing Gordon brought her."

Kathy pulled out the pad and began writing him a note. Logan read it, then nodded. "Well, I never met anyone who

194

needed protection less than Tess, but I'll watch out for her," he said, his eyes direct on Tess. "But why do you think she needs protection?"

Kathy bent over the pad again, scribbling again. "Do you have photos of the clothing the victims of the serial killer wore?"

Logan showed the note to Tess. "Of course. Why?"

"They wore blue," Kathy wrote without answering Tess's question.

Tess sat down and researched on her iPhone, flipping through notes and photos. Then she looked up. "I've got them," she said.

"Let me see," Kathy wrote.

Tess held out the phone and watched her aunt study the photos. Then Kathy picked up the pen and pad again. "Not sure. Been years. Need you to go to the shop."

Logan touched her hand. "What's this about, Kathy?"

"Need you to go to the shop," she wrote on the pad. "No one can know." She turned to Tess and gestured for her to open the drawer on the bedside table.

Tess pulled out her aunt's purse and handed it to her. Kathy searched in it and produced a key. She handed it to Tess and had her return the purse to the table.

"Look in the back of the storage closet," she wrote on the pad. "There's a bag of scraps from the quilt. Take them to state lab. Top secret. Do DNA."

Logan felt a chill. "Whose DNA will we find, Kathy?"

"I hope I'm wrong," she wrote. "I think from the women who were killed."

Then she leaned down and picked up the quilt and held it out to them.

"Kathy, you're not saying you killed these girls?" Logan asked very carefully.

She shook her head violently, then dropped the pad to clutch her head and moan.

"Gordon brought her items of clothing to make that quilt," Tess said slowly. "He said they were from his sisters."

Logan stared at Kathy. "You realize what you're saying? You suspect that Gordon might have killed them?"

"And Sam?" Tess said. Her hand flew to her mouth. "He might have killed Sam?"

She stood and swayed. Logan jumped to his feet and put his hands on her arms.

"I'm okay," she insisted, but her color was ghastly and her eyes huge, the pupils dilated.

Then she slapped her hand to her mouth and rushed to the bathroom, slamming the door behind her.

Logan followed her and winced when he heard retching.

"Tess! Let me in."

"I'm all right!" she called out.

When she emerged, she held a damp washcloth to her cheek. "Dry heaves. It was just the shock."

She walked over to her chair and picked something up from the floor before she sat.

"Aunt Kathy, I—I don't know what to say."

She wrote on the pad and held it up. "I hope I'm wrong."

Tess checked her watch. "The shop is closing in half an hour. Be best to go after everyone's gone home, so there are no questions. Since she gave us the key, we don't have to worry about a search warrant."

"Well," Logan said after a moment. He looked at Tess. "Talk about a stunner. Imagine if you put the pieces together after all this time."

Kathy lay back against her pillows, looking spent. She glanced over at Tess and held out her hand. When Tess didn't understand, she pointed at a piece of fabric that lay on her bed.

Tess gave it to her aunt, who then handed it to Logan. He stared at the piece of material with an appliqué of a figure of a girl in a silky blue dress. She carried a shawl and walked under trees near the St. Augustine lighthouse.

"The square just triggered something," Tess told him. "Then I put it down on the bed while I went to see about Aunt Kathy's meds and when I came back, I looked at the blue memory quilt. Something clicked. She noticed it, too. Comes from being a cop's wife, I guess."

When Logan handed Tess back the square, she folded it up and tucked it into her tote. Then she went still.

"Tess? You okay?"

She made a sound he didn't understand. He got up and walked over to her, wondering if she was feeling sick again. He picked up the wastepaper basket and brought it to her.

"Roses," she said, staring with wide eyes at the dark blooms.

"Yeah, who threw away perfectly good flowers?" he asked.

"Gordon brought them for Aunt Kathy," Tess told him. "She wrote they were 'doghouse flowers' and threw them into the trash."

She reached into the container and pulled out a rose, wincing and sucking on her finger when a thorn must have pricked her.

"Red rose," she said and looked up at Logan.

"Yes, it's a red rose," he said, wondering where this was leading.

"I found one at the wax museum, remember? Near Machiavelli."

He nodded and waited, watching the play of emotions on her face as she processed something. "Remember how Gordon said something about Machiavelli at the barbecue?"

"I remember. Does this have something to do with the serial killer case?"

"Maybe. Maybe not."

She tapped some keys on her iPhone again and bit her lip. "I can't find anything . . . I just don't think it's a coincidence he talked about a prince and it says here that's Machiavelli's most famous book. *The Prince*."

"I still don't get the connection."

"There may not be one. But there's something . . ."

"Trust your gut," he said.

"We still have a little time to kill before we go to the quilt shop. Let's go by the museum."

Logan glanced at Kathy and saw that she was fading, the energy she'd spent trying to communicate taking its toll on top of the surgery the day before. Tess fussed over her, getting a blanket from the closet and tucking it around her shoulders. Neither of the women looked at the quilt lying at the foot of the bed. Kathy was out in minutes. As soon as Tess was sure she was asleep, she bundled the quilt into a plastic bag that held scraps in her tote bag and they left the room.

Tess stopped at the nurse's station to say that she'd be back in a while. They rode down in the elevator without speaking. When the doors slid open, Tess pulled out her cell and dialed a number. "I need a sec," she told Logan. "Claudia? Hi, I need a favor. Can you come sit with Aunt Kathy at the hospital while I take care of some work? I really don't want to leave her right now. You can? Great! Room 220."

"Maybe now you can worry a little less."

Tess smiled at Logan. "Maybe."

They didn't talk as they drove to the museum. There, Tess introduced herself and Logan and asked the manager on duty if they could look around.

"Have you caught whoever broke in that night?" the woman asked Tess.

She shook her head. "Sorry. There was a witness who said he saw a teenager running from the building and heard the alarm went off. We haven't had any good leads. I'd just like to take a look again, if you don't mind."

"Sure."

Tess went straight to the figure of Machiavelli. She stared up into his face as if she hoped he'd say something to her.

"This the guy you found the rose in front of?" Logan asked her.

"Yeah. Handsome, isn't he?"

Logan shifted and looked at her askance. "I wouldn't know." He shoved his hands in his pockets and rocked back on his heels as she studied the figure.

"High cheekbones. An arrogant air. Dark, mysterious eyes. Bet he was quite a hit with the ladies." She glanced at him. "Hope I'm not making you jealous," she said and chuckled.

"Ah, so you've fallen for our Niccolo," said a guide as she came to stand beside them. "Yes, he had looks, intelligence, and charm. Oh, and wealth and political connections."

"You know a lot about him, eh?"

"I know a little about every one of the figures. His most famous work was *The Prince*."

Tess turned to her. "Give me the Cliffs Notes on that."

The woman laughed. "Quick synopsis without reading it, eh? Okay. Well, he was a master manipulator, using his power and influence to advance himself politically. He believed the ends justified the means."

That got Logan's attention. He jerked his head to stare at Tess, and she nodded.

The guide went on to talk about the life and times of Machiavelli. Logan found his attention drawn to the figure of a woman that stood nearby.

"So this is what the infamous Lucretia Borgia looked like," Logan mused. "She was a stunner." He glanced over at Tess and grinned, teasing her for her admiration of Machiavelli's looks.

"A contemporary of Machiavelli," said the guide. "Historians have implied that she engaged in political intrigue and used a special ring to poison an adversary but nothing was ever proven."

"Unless you see the crime committed, you can't charge the perp," murmured Tess. She frowned as she leaned closer to look at Machiavelli's hand. "What happened to his ring finger? Mob hit?"

The guide laughed. "No, we've just had some vandalism through the years. Someone broke off the finger to get the reproduction ring he wore. We've had a new hand made for him, and the ring is just wax now. It has a neat symbol on it that reminds me of the lions at the Bridge of Lions. Would you like to see it?"

Tess glanced at her watch. "We just have a few minutes before we have to be someplace . . ."

"It's right over here in my office."

He expected an office filled with wax heads and stuff, but it was a normal business office with a desk loaded with books and papers. The guide quickly found the book she was looking for and flipped through the pages. "Here we are."

Logan and Tess stared at the image of an elegant M and a lion. It was the same M found on each of the bodies of victims of the serial killer.

19

"Don't know how you stood being in that place at night," Logan said as they got into the car to go to Tess's aunt's shop. "It reminded me of that movie. *Mystery of the Wax Museum.* So creepy. There were these wax figures that seemed to have human eyes following them around."

"I know the feeling," she said dryly.

"Oh, yeah, guess you did." He shivered. "Did you get the code for the alarm? Wouldn't want our fellow officers showing up to see who broke in."

"No fear. I got it."

Once there, Tess quickly located the supply closet her aunt had mentioned, pulled on plastic gloves, and after a few minutes found the bag of scraps in the rear of it. Logan donned plastic gloves and pulled a sheet of plastic from an evidence bag he'd brought. He spread it out on one of the fabric cutting tables.

Tess carefully pulled clothing items from the bag, gasping when she found a length of blue satin.

"What is it?"

"Sam had this shawl at the prom."

"You're sure?"

"It was my shawl. My dress. She borrowed it." She stared, shocked, as tears slipped down her cheeks.

"Stay with me, Tess. Don't lose it now."

She gulped back her tears, placing each of the clothing items on the plastic, and Logan began taking photos.

"You thinking what I'm thinking?" she asked, her voice echoing in the silent shop.

"Victim two was last seen wearing a blue cotton blouse. Victim four, a jacket of blue and white flowers."

"Aunt Kathy said blue was Gordon's mother's favorite color."

Logan looked at her. "What?"

"Blue was Gordon's mother's favorite color."

"Wonder if that's why he fixated on it. Mother issues."

After he'd taken photos, Tess carefully folded each item and put it in an evidence bag.

"That's it."

Logan nodded, stripped off his gloves, and put the camera back in its case. Tess wrote notes on each of the bags, then reached for a big paper shopping bag and placed the evidence bags inside.

"Good idea," he said. "Just in case anyone is outside and wonders about us carrying evidence bags out."

Tess glanced around, careful to make sure she'd closed the supply closet, and they hadn't left any sign they'd been inside the shop. All seemed so normal: there were bolts of fabric, craft kits for purchase, and quilts on the wall. Christmas projects were already on display, inviting customers to make their plans for gifts and get their supplies in time to make them for the upcoming holiday season.

She set the alarm before they left the shop and locked the front door. "Okay, you have the address of the state lab. Give me a call when you get there. My friend said she'll keep this top secret and start on it tonight. Oh, and don't forget to use the name I gave you. We don't want Gordon finding out."

Logan nodded. "Where will you be?"

"I'm going to go sit with Aunt Kathy. And don't worry. If I see Gordon, I won't let anything slip."

"Be careful."

"I will."

He dropped her off at her house. But before she could get out he pulled her over and gave her a hard kiss. "Promise me you'll be careful, if he comes around."

"Don't worry about that. I don't intend on being in the same room with him. Call me when you get back, okay?"

She got out of the car, watched him back out, and waved before she went into the house. Restless, she fixed a cup of tea and pulled out her phone to study the photos she'd taken, alongside the ones Logan had photographed with the evidence camera.

They'd need the DNA to prove the clothing had belonged to the victims, but it would take time and she wasn't sure they had time. Who knew when the killer—whether it was Gordon or someone else—would murder again?

She had the names, phone numbers, and addresses of the family members of the victims. It took just a few minutes, and she'd set up times she could stop by to talk to three of them. She heard the question in the voices, but simply said she wanted to talk to them. No one refused her. Everyone wanted justice for their loved one.

One by one she received positive identification of a clothing item from a victim's relative.

"I can't tell you anything more," she said repeatedly. "And I need your promise you won't say a word to anyone. Not anyone, not another relative, not a spouse, or significant other," she emphasized. "We don't want the case compromised."

"But you have a suspect at last," Thad Masters said, sighing heavily.

Tess felt such a surge of sympathy for the man. He'd aged so much since his daughter's murder.

She touched his arm. "Promise me."

"No one will hear it from my lips."

Tess drove on to the hospital, stopping to get a takeout meal for herself and a milkshake for her aunt. She wasn't sure if Aunt Kathy could drink it with her wired jaw, but figured she'd ask a nurse when she got there.

"Well, hey, Tess, how are you?"

She jumped, then turned to see Pam, the chief's wife, walking toward her.

"You okay, honey? Seem kind of edgy."

Tess managed a laugh. "I'm fine. How's Jeremy?" Pam frowned. "It's the weirdest thing. Doctor said the blood work showed his potassium is way, way above normal."

They walked into the hospital lobby, and Pam pressed the elevator button.

"I thought we needed potassium," Tess said, trying to remember what she'd read about it.

"Apparently it can be a poison," Pam said as they stepped into the elevator. "If you get too much it can cause a heart attack. He's still not out of danger, but at least we know now what was making him sick. And maybe we can figure out how he came to have too much of it in his system."

Pam glanced at the food in Tess's hands. "Who are you here to see?"

"Aunt Kathy."

"Oh, that's right, Jeremy told me she lost her balance and fell." When Tess didn't respond, Pam looked at her. "Did I get that wrong?"

Tess felt put between a rock and a hard place. "I'm not sure. All I know is she had to have her jaw wired."

"Poor thing. I'll stop and see her after I see Jeremy. Listen, why don't you stop up for just a minute and say hi? Jeremy's feeling pretty low since he's been out of work for a week and all."

She was starving, her aunt's milkshake was melting, but who turned down a request from the boss's wife? "Sure. I'd love to."

The chief didn't look as happy as his wife had said he'd be when he saw Tess. Then she saw it wasn't her he was looking away from, but his wife. He tried to hide a cup of coffee from a local coffee house, but there was nowhere to put it.

"Busted," said his wife. She folded her arms across her chest and glared at him. "You know you're not allowed to have that for a while. Who brought it to you?"

"No one," he said. "Hi, Tess."

"Hi." She told herself it wasn't very nice of her to enjoy seeing him looking a little intimidated by his angry wife.

"Give it to me," Pam said, walking over to hold out her hand.

"Aw, it's just a little coffee," he protested. "And think about how much it cost him."

"Him?" She looked at Tess, then her husband. "This smells like one of your work buddies."

"So, Tess, how is Kathy doing?"

It was an obvious attempt to change the subject, but Tess grabbed onto it, seeing it as a way to get out of the room. She held up the milkshake. "She's doing pretty well, but I'm taking this to her now since she can't eat regular food yet with her jaw wired."

"Well, tell her we hope she's feeling better real soon."

"Hope you do, too." Tess turned to leave. She stopped at the door. Should she tell him what she and Logan suspected? But they had no real proof yet. It was a big accusation she had no way of backing up.

"Tess?"

She turned around. "Nothing. I'll tell Gordon not to get you any more coffee."

"Aw, now, don't be getting him into trouble," Jeremy said. "I asked him—" he stopped and shut his mouth when Pam gave him a look.

If he only knew what she and Logan had been up to that afternoon . . .

Claudia had promised that she'd stay until Tess returned to the hospital. Gordon had acted like he would be too busy to visit again that day. But if Jeremy was sipping coffee did that mean that Gordon had come back?

She got off the elevator and approached her aunt's room with some trepidation. When she pushed open the door, she saw that her aunt lay sleeping. Claudia sat in a chair beside her, her knitting needles clicking away.

Tess tiptoed in and put her food and the milkshake on the bedside table. "How's she doing?"

"Fell asleep about an hour ago." Claudia tucked her knitting in her tote bag, stood and stretched. "You let me know if you need me to sit with her again."

"I will. Thank you." She hugged the woman, then settled into the chair and pulled her dinner from the bag along with her notepad and pen in case her aunt woke up.

Tess had just taken a bite out of her tuna sandwich when the door opened abruptly. "Hello, Tess."

She looked up at the familiar voice. Gordon stood in the doorway.

Logan tried calling Tess at the next red light he had to stop at a few miles from St. Augustine.

The call went straight to voicemail.

It wasn't like her not to pick up. He wondered if her aunt was having a problem. But if she were, he figured Tess would have called him. He checked the time. Certainly, it was possible she'd gone home and was sleeping. There was nothing more he wanted right now. Well, he'd like to see her before he went home, but if that wasn't possible, then of course, he'd settle for knowing she was all right.

He drove past her house, and her car wasn't in the driveway. She must still be at the hospital. He headed in that direction and sure enough, he found it was parked in the visitor section.

While he wished she'd been able to go home, it did give him the opportunity to see her again and for that he was grateful. The hospital's main entrance was locked for the night so he went in through the emergency room entrance, showed a security guard his badge, and was directed to an elevator that took him to Kathy's floor.

She was sitting up in bed looking a little better than she had earlier. A takeout cup from an ice cream shop Tess loved sat in front of her on her bed table. She smiled and waved to him.

"Where's Tess?"

When she looked confused and shook her head, he pulled out his notepad and pen and handed them to her.

"I woke up and thought she'd stepped outside with you," she wrote. "She must just have stepped out of the room." She glanced in the direction of the restroom door.

Logan walked over to it but since the door was ajar, he knew he wouldn't find her there.

Kathy waved a hand. "Isn't that her dinner?" she wrote on the pad.

"Don't know. I had an errand to run," he explained as he walked over and examined the take-out dinner that had been barely touched. "But yeah, that's got to be her food. I don't know anyone else who puts potato chips inside her sandwich before eating."

It was then he saw the napkin that lay just underneath the Styrofoam container. On it was one word—a name: Andy.

Andy. What did that name mean? Why had Tess written it on the napkin?

Logan racked his brain. The name seemed familiar but he couldn't remember why.

Andy. He paced the room, returned to stare at the napkin.

He glancd at Kathy when she picked up the TV remote and turned on the news.

Logan felt punched in the gut.

"Kathy, did Gordon stop by?" he asked casually as he turned his back for a moment, picked up the napkin, and tucked it inside his shirt pocket.

When he turned around, he saw she was shaking her head. "Just Claudia, Pam—Chief's wife—and Tess."

He nodded, careful not to show the dread he was feeling. But he needed to get moving and find Tess. Gordon had her, and he doubted it was for a chat about work. She wouldn't have scribbled "Andy" and left it there with an uneaten dinner.

"I'm going to go find her," he told Kathy. "She might be out at the nurse's station or down the hall making a phone call. I'll be right back."

He didn't find her anywhere. His heart raced.

What did you do when you suspected the police chief of murder—and he had the woman you loved?

Logan went to the nurse's station and asked her to page whoever was in charge of security for the shift. In just a few minutes, the man was striding down the hall.

"Kevin Sanders. How can I help you?"

He showed his badge and asked if he could see the security tape of the hallway and elevator.

"Can you tell me what this is about?"

He measured the man and went with his gut. "One of our officers is missing. She was last seen here visiting a patient."

"Come to my office." Once there, he sat and began tapping at the keyboard of his computer.

It took a few minutes but Logan had his answer: there was Tess walking down the hall with Gordon. She appeared calm, as if nothing were wrong. The time stamp showed her walking past just twenty minutes before. Logan felt the first surge of hope. The shorter the time from her going missing, the stronger the chance he could find her alive.

"Can I get a closeup?"

When the image of Tess's face was enlarged, Logan saw the truth as she glanced at what she must have seen was a security camera: there was a trace of fear in her eyes but her chin was lifted high. She was showing determination to the man she walked beside.

"The hospital entrance," Logan said tersely. "Can you give me a view of the entrance a few minutes after this?"

But there were no images of Tess leaving the hospital with Gordon.

"What about other entrances?"

Sanders was texting on his cell. "I'm asking the guards at the other entrances. We should have a response very quickly."

Logan met his gaze. Nothing was quick enough.

"I'll be right outside." He stepped outside the office, pulled out his cell, and called a friend on the force.

"I need a favor," he began. "I need you to ping Tess's cell phone. And please, no jokes about me stalking her."

Fortunately, Ed didn't joke, and he didn't fool around. The last location was the hospital Logan stood in.

Logan slammed a hand against the wall.

"You want me to check there for you? I can go there now."

"I'm already here," Logan said tersely.

"Can I ask a question?"

"If I can answer it, I will."

"Is Gordon looking for her?"

Logan hadn't expected a question like that. "I can't answer that."

There was a pause. "Do you want me to meet you at the hospital?"

Once again, Logan was faced with having to trust someone he didn't feel he knew as well as he'd like—with something as monumental as Tess's safety.

"Yeah," he said. "How soon can you get here?"

"Ten minutes."

"No lights, no siren. I'm in the security chief's office on the first floor. Ask for Kevin Sanders if you have any trouble finding it."

He walked back into the security office. "What's the word?"

"No one's seen her leave. Doesn't mean she didn't. But most of the security staff here knows Tess, and they didn't see her."

He told himself maybe Gordon still didn't know about their suspicions. Maybe he and Tess were in the hospital cafeteria having coffee. Tess was a smart woman. She wouldn't jump the gun and confront him.

Logan told himself maybe he was just in denial that something bad had happened to Tess.

"I asked a fellow officer to ping her cell, and the location of the last call came from here in the hospital," Logan told Jason. "That could either mean she made her last call from here or she's still here."

"Just say the word, and we'll do a floor-by-floor search."

"Do it." Logan had a photo of Tess he'd taken on the sailboat that day before she'd gotten sick. He sent it to Sanders to use for the search.

"No one's to make contact with her—especially if she's with anyone."

"Got it. Wait, got a text coming in. She's in the cafeteria. Whitney says she's with a guy."

"Get a description," Logan said tersely.

Sanders tapped at the keyboard of his cell and looked up. "Fiftyish. Crew-cut."

"It's Gordon."

"So, does that mean everything's okay?"

"No," Logan said. "Don't stand down. I'll call you as soon as I can."

And he was out the door.

20

Tess felt her stomach knot the moment Gordon walked into her Aunt Kathy's room.

"I thought you weren't going to be able to come back today."

He walked in and glanced at his wife. "Taking a break. How's she doing?"

"The nurse gave her more pain meds an hour or so ago. I don't think she'll wake up for a while."

She hoped he'd do his usual duty visit and leave quickly, but he lingered.

"What are you eating there?"

"Tuna sandwich."

He made a face. "I feel like a steak. Want to join me?"

She'd rather climb into a shark tank and be eaten. "No, but thanks. I think I'll head on home, since the nurse doesn't expect Aunt Kathy to wake up tonight."

Then his attention shifted. He walked over and frowned when he saw the roses he'd brought lying in the wastepaper basket. "What are these doing in here?"

"You'd have to ask your wife."

His eyes narrowed. "What are you saying?"

She took a breath and met his gaze. "I think you know."

"No, why don't you tell me."

Tess wiped her hands on a napkin. "I haven't said anything before. But it's time. It's time you stopped hurting my aunt."

"Did she tell you that?" he thundered.

"Ssh!" she hissed. "You'll wake her up." She met his stormy gaze. "You know she's not going to talk against you. Abusers count on that."

"This is none of your business."

"You made it my business when you raised your hand against her," she said quietly. "I'm sworn to serve and protect and not just some citizen on the block. It includes my family. I'm going to do everything I can to make sure my aunt doesn't get hurt again."

He walked over to stand before her, the table her dinner sat on the only thing keeping him from coming closer. "She's not going to leave me." He folded his arms over his beefy chest and glared at her.

There was a knock on the door. A nurse walked in with her computer on a rolling cart. "Visiting hours are over in a few minutes."

Gordon quickly wiped the anger from his expression and turned to flash a smile at the woman. "Sorry, I just came from the station. Wanted to see the wife before I headed home."

"Oh, I didn't realize it was you." The nurse gave him a big smile. "I suppose we can make an exception and let you stay a little longer."

"No, no," he said magnanimously. "I wouldn't want you to give me special treatment. C'mon, Tess, what do you say to a steak?"

Her appetite gone, she closed the top on the Styrofoam container. "No, thanks, like I said, I want to go home."

"Well, coffee then," he said, using a persuasive tone, his eyes on the nurse as she took his wife's vital signs. "We'll finish our discussion."

Tess told herself he was playing her under the benevolent gaze of the nurse. But maybe she could talk him into counseling . . . at the very least, persuading him he and Aunt Kathy should take a little time away from each other.

The nurse finished up and turned to leave. And as she did, Tess caught Gordon giving her an assessing glance. Tess frowned, angry he looked at another woman like that with his injured wife lying just a few feet from him.

Then ice ran in her veins as she remembered her and Logan's suspicions.

She didn't want to be left in the room with him again. While he was preoccupied with the nurse, she quietly reached for her pen and scribbled on the napkin she'd placed on her lap. Then she pushed it just under the edge of the Styrofoam container.

So she'd go downstairs to the cafeteria and have coffee with Gordon. Maybe she was a crazy optimist about thinking she'd talk him into counseling. In any event, she wouldn't be in this small room with him. When Logan returned, she'd be able to walk away and find out what had happened at the state lab.

"Let's get that coffee," she said and she stood.

Gordon nodded, so sure of her acceptance that he didn't bother to look in her direction.

They went through the line for their coffee and found a table. Gordon reached into his pocket and pulled out a packet of sugar that he ripped open and dumped into his coffee.

"You carry your own sugar?"

"I'm tired of only finding the fake stuff on the table," he said. "So where's Logan?"

"Watching some game on TV."

"Which one?"

215

She shrugged. "Who knows. He loves ESPN." Her coffee tasted bitter. She chose a pink packet of sweetener and stirred it into the coffee.

Coffee. The chief said that Gordon had brought him coffee. He did that at the station a lot.

She glanced up and found Gordon watching her. It was a little unnerving the way he did it. She told herself to relax and act natural. No way was she letting him know that she suspected him of anything.

"I'd like you to consider counseling," she began. "I know someone who—"

"That again?" he snapped. "Like I said, it's none of your business."

"When we were in Aunt Kathy's room, you said we could talk about it."

He shrugged and let his eyes roam around the room. Then he tensed. Tess followed the line of his look and saw a security guard at the periphery of the room. The man glanced around the room, then in their direction, before moving on.

Tess wouldn't have thought anything of it, but then she caught a glimpse of another passing by the entrance of the cafeteria.

"What's going on?" Gordon asked her.

"Don't know. Shift change? Listen, I really want to talk about you and Aunt Kathy—"

His eyes hardened. "Subject's closed. And don't go trying to influence Kathy. Maybe you've forgotten who you're working for now."

Shocked, she could only stare at him for a long moment. "Are you threatening me?"

"Why no," he said, smiling coldly at her. "I think you're smart enough not to do something stupid like try to cause your superior problems, aren't you?"

He glanced over at the entrance. "Well, well, look who's here."

⊱≺≻⊰

Tess felt relief wash over her as Logan strode toward their table but tried to school her expression. Gordon wasn't going to suspect what she and Logan had been doing that day if she had her way.

"I didn't think I'd see you again tonight," she said, smiling at him. "Tired of watching ESPN?"

"Never," he said, acknowledging Gordon with a nod.

"What game were you watching?" Gordon asked him.

"I fell asleep," Logan told him.

"If you were so tired, why'd you come here?"

"I wanted to see Tess. And the Chief. Oh, and Kathy. Put your hands on the table where we can see them, Gordon. You're under arrest."

"For what? Kathy's not pressing charges against me," Gordon blustered. "And *I'm* Chief now while Jeremy is incapacitated."

"Yeah, wonder how much you had to do with that, too," Logan said. "You're under arrest for the murder of two women, Samantha Marshall and Toni Sanchez to start. We expect to file more charges in the next few days."

"Murder? On what evidence?"

"Remember the quilt?" Tess asked him. "Years ago, you asked Aunt Kathy to make a quilt from the clothing you brought her."

"That was from my sisters."

"Some of it. But we've already had two items positively identified by family."

"You took the quilt to the families and had them say pieces of it belonged to their relatives?" he laughed, incredulous.

217

"We found the clothing. Aunt Kathy kept it all these years. You see, quilters seldom throw perfectly good fabric away."

"Kathy had the clothing and you're accusing me?" Gordon scoffed. "That'll never hold up in court."

"Chief seems to think it will. There'll be DNA from the victims on the clothing. Only the killer would have that clothing."

"Enough talk, Gordon." Logan said. "Put your hands on the table where we can see them."

The cafeteria was a little noisy but there was no mistaking the sound of a gun being cocked.

Gordon smiled. "Yes, and it's trained on Tess."

"Haven't you killed enough?" Logan asked, berating himself for not anticipating the man's actions.

Gordon looked at Tess. "Let's go."

She shook her head. "I'm not going anywhere with you, Gordon. Give it up."

He glanced to his left. "Take a look at that kid, Tess. And that old woman at the next table. You willing to risk them?"

Logan watched her head turn slowly and take in the sight of the little boy dipping French fries into a pool of ketchup on his plate. The old woman sat tiredly stirring a cup of tea, her walker propped beside her.

"Don't listen to him, Tess."

She waved her hand at him. "Where are you going to go, Gordon? No one's going to let you go anywhere. Get a good lawyer and fight the charges."

"Let's go, Tess. And don't try anything. Remember, I taught you everything you know."

A trickle of sweat ran cold down Logan's back as he watched her stand. Gordon stood as well, quickly slipped his hand holding his weapon in his jacket pocket, and wrapped his arm around her waist. A look of revulsion crossed her face. She shifted her gaze to Logan, and her chin lifted.

"Not a victim," it seemed to say. He wanted to nod but didn't dare as Gordon kept his eye on him while he moved Tess toward the door.

Something shifted in the periphery of Logan's vision. A security guard stood on the far side of the room waiting for direction. He inclined his head toward the doorway where Logan saw Ed.

And Gordon didn't.

But there were too many people in the room. Logan knew—*knew*—at a deep gut level—if he acted and someone got hurt Tess would never forgive him. Or herself.

Suddenly, Tess was snatching up a walker sitting beside a table and smashing it over Gordon's head, hitting him several times and then trapping him in the metal frame as he lay on the floor.

Diners screamed and began diving under tables and rushing from the room.

Logan ran to help her as she threw herself on Gordon as he fought back, his head bloody. A shot rang out, and she slumped on top of him but before Logan got to her, she was beating at Gordon with her fists, beating at the hand that held the gun until she captured it.

She fought him as he dragged her off Gordon. The security guard and Ed rushed to immobilize Gordon, pulling the mangled walker off him, flipping him over and snapping handcuffs on him.

"Machiavelli," she scoffed, breathing hard as Logan held onto her for dear life. "Gordon, you're nothing but a pathetic excuse for a man."

Logan held her steady when she sagged against him. "Thanks," she said at last.

"For what? You saved yourself."

She stared at him, her face white. "For pulling me off him. I wanted to kill him. I never felt like that before."

Logan pushed her hair back with hands that shook. "He killed your friend and we don't know how many other women. He hurt your aunt. And I have a suspicion he's been making the Chief sick. I'm glad *I* didn't get my hands on him."

She rested her forehead on his. "It's for the courts to punish him. And he'll answer to God one day."

Sighing, she drew away and grimaced. "I need to go apologize to that poor woman whose walker I ruined."

"Sit down," he said, pushing her into a chair. "I'll go talk to her. Let me do one thing for you, okay?"

Tess stared at him. "You did more than one," she said quietly. "I knew I could rely on you. That made it possible for me to keep looking for a way out."

He found himself smiling. "You can always rely on me. I've got your back, partner."

"Well, we had some excitement tonight, didn't we?" the woman said as Logan walked up to her with the mangled walker in his hands.

"We did indeed. Are you okay?"

She nodded. "It'll take more than that to rattle me. I raised six sons who were always walloping each other. What did that man do?"

"We arrested him for murdering several young women. He was trying to take my partner with him to avoid going to jail."

"Ah. Well, your partner sure beat the stuffing out of him for trying to do that, didn't she? Good for her. Just shows women can take care of themselves."

Logan grinned. "Yes, ma'am. She wants me to apologize to you for appropriating your walker. I'm sending one of our officers to borrow you one from the hospital. I'll bring you a new walker tomorrow."

She reached for the walker and tried to pull out a bent leg. Logan did his best to help her but it wouldn't cooperate.

"I'm afraid it's a goner," he told her. "I guess we can say it died in the line of duty."

"That's a shame. Would have been quite the conversation piece to take to the senior center."

He was glad to see an officer wheeling a new walker to the table.

"Why, thank you, young man," the woman told him.

"My pleasure, ma'am. And Officer Jenkins here will see you out to your car."

"I'm sure going to have a story for the ladies at the bridge game at the senior center," he heard her say as he returned to Tess.

"Ready to go?" he asked her.

"I wish you meant home," she said. "That's hours off. We have reports to do." She sighed. "First, I need to go talk to my aunt."

She still looked a little in shock to him, but it was the right thing to do. He was proud of her for wanting to do it.

"How about you do that, and I'll go give a quick report to the Chief?"

"Deal."

Logan left her at her aunt's room and checked in with the Chief. When he returned to get Tess, she was still sitting by her aunt's bed, holding her hand, talking quietly to her, while Kathy cried.

He'd passed by the chapel on the same floor earlier when he'd been looking for Tess. There hadn't been time to go inside and pray for His help. He'd done it on the run and hoped He'd understand and go before him to save Tess. Now it was time to say thanks.

The small chapel was empty, and he was grateful for the chance to sit and look at the stained glass window illuminated by a soft light behind it. Jesus sat in a field surrounded by his flock, a gentle-looking shepherd watching over it. Tess had been watched over—*he'd* been watched over that night.

An evil man had a plan, but God had a greater one: helping bring justice here until divine justice could prevail.

And God had a plan for him, Logan realized. He'd been led here to meet an amazing woman who had helped him realize he'd strayed in his faith. He bent his head, thanked God, and felt His peace settle on him.

He became aware someone had come into the chapel a few minutes later. He opened his eyes and turned, intending to leave so they might have the same time to reflect in solitude. Tess stood a few feet from him. He held out his hand, and she walked forward to take it and sit beside him.

"I was going to the Chief's room to get you and thought I'd come in here and say a thank you prayer first."

"We thought alike. Do you want some time alone?"

She shook her head slowly, looking deep into his eyes. "No, I'd like you to be here when I say thanks to Him for helping me tonight. And for sending you to me."

"So you're feeling His plan for us, too?" he asked carefully, his heart beating faster.

She nodded. "I love you."

He touched her cheek. "I think I started falling in love with you the first day I met you. Marry me, Tess. Here."

Tess looked up at the stained glass window, then at him. She smiled. "Here."

Discussion Questions

Please don't read before completing the book, as the questions contain spoilers!

1. Tess Villanova has spent most of her adult life in a passionate pursuit for justice for her best friend. Do you believe her friend would have wanted her to do this? Why or why not?

2. When Tess meets a man who seems to support who and what she is, she finds herself putting up defenses. Do you think she secretly doesn't believe she's worthy? Have you ever felt you're not worthy of someone's love and respect?

3. Tess uses quilting to relax and to work out a problem in her professional life. What do you use to help you relax? How do you problem-solve? Do you craft or have a hobby? What is it? Why were you drawn to it?

4. Logan McMillan is looking for a new start in a new city. Have you ever moved thinking that something will be different but found the move was geographic and you didn't find the change you hoped for? What did you do?

5. Tess and Logan both blame God for the loss of best friends. Have you ever blamed God for making you unhappy? What was the situation? How did you cope? Did you eventually change your mind about being angry with God? How did you do this?

6. Tess's aunt has become a mother figure and her uncle a mentor, but she suspects that he is hurting her aunt. What would you do in a similar situation? Do you know someone who is being abused? Have you tried to help her or him?

7. Both Tess and Logan are committed to their jobs to the point some might call them workaholics. Are you? How do you force yourself to back away from work to have something more in your life?

8. Tess doesn't believe in ghosts, but sometimes she feels her life has been haunted by an event beyond her control. Have you ever had something change your life and affect you for years? How did you handle it?

9. When a woman is murdered, suspicion falls on a homeless man. Like many cities, Tess's community has struggled with how to solve homelessness. How is your community working—or not working—to eliminate homelessness?

10. When Tess invites Logan to attend her church, he jokes that the walls might fall down because he hasn't attended a church in a long time. How do you feel about what he says? Do you think God listens to you? When did you feel He didn't? What did you do?

11. Sometimes bad things happen to good people. How do you think God used Sam's death for good in Tess's life?

12. Logan realizes that God had a plan for him in the midst of the sadness he felt when his friend died. He moves to St. Augustine and finds purpose in his new job, helps to solve a crime, and meets Tess. What do you feel is God's plan for you?

Want to learn more about author
Barbara Cameron and check out other great
fiction from Abingdon Press?

Sign up for our fiction newsletter at
www.AbingdonPress.com
to read interviews with your favorite authors, find tips
for starting a reading group, and stay posted on what
new titles are on the horizon. It's a place to connect
with other fiction readers or post a
comment about this book.

Be sure to visit Barbara online!

www.BarbaraCameron.com
www.AmishLiving.com

We hope you enjoyed *Scraps of Evidence* and that you will continue to read the Quilts of Love series of books from Abingdon Press. Here's an excerpt from Linda S. Clare's *A Sky Without Stars*.

Prologue

Pine Ridge, South Dakota
Frankie Chasing Bear

I did not come to quilt-making easily. The urge to piece together shapes and colors wasn't my gift.

But when I was twelve, Grandmother said soon the quilt might be all that was left of what we once were. By the time your children wrap quilts around themselves, she told me, the star and all it stands for may be a dim memory, lit only by the fire of ancestors, clouded by ruddy smoke hanging in the sky.

Grandmother's face was crisscrossed with fine lines showing off sharp cheekbones, a strong square jaw, hard work. A silvery gray braid, straight as the truth, hung down her back. I tried to make my stitches as small and even as hers, but my childish hands proved slow and awkward. She said I only needed practice and showed me again: up, pulled through, and down.

Just before she died, Grandmother and I sat together one last time. She stopped to smooth a small wrinkle in the quilt top. "Lakota were favored among tribes," she said. "Our people stood at the top of the hills. The buffalo and the deer bowed to our warriors and we lived together in peace. The peace pipe showed us how to live and the stars helped us find good hunting grounds."

Grandmother had told the story a thousand times, but I didn't interrupt. I was fighting the thread again, scribbled into a hopeless knot. She looked up and said, "Keep the thread short." I obeyed.

Her brown fingers reminded me of an old tree branch, but they deftly worked the needle: up, pulled through and down, up, through and down. "One day, the sun rose on white men. They brought their religion, but they often did not listen to their God's teachings." She paused to watch my crooked stitches take shape, nodding when I got them even. "We were brought low and herded like animals."

Again the nod of approval for my efforts. "They had no explanation, except to point to their Book. We were to love their God and love each other."

Grandmother laughed. "Lakota need no instruction on love." Tears glistened in her tired black eyes. She'd seen something terrible in the smoke, she said for the hundredth time. A red rose, unopened. Blood, a river of blood. Another day was coming, she said, when words from the Book would take place: *We were considered as sheep to be slaughtered.*

I dared not remind her she prayed to the God of the Bible. That she stood in two worlds, fully Lakota, fully Christian. I worry it's not possible for me. Indians who go to the church are shunned by their kin and by the whites. Outcasts, their feet in no world at all.

Before we traveled to Arizona, Grandmother made me promise to make this Lakota Star for my son. Sew love into every stitch and remember: abed without a quilt is like a sky without stars. The quilt will help this child remember who he is, she said. The star will tell him how much he is loved and the light will save him at the last day.

1

Mid-August 1951
Outside Phoenix, Arizona

Frankie Chasing Bear eased the old Chevy pickup to the side of the rutted dirt road. If she hadn't run out of quilting thread, they'd have stayed home on a day this hot. A plume of steam rose from the radiator and disappeared into the pale sun-bleached sky.

She slapped the steering wheel with the heel of her hand. "Not again!" A stab of guilt penetrated deep, an ache she'd carried since Hank's death. At the time, leaving South Dakota for the West seemed to be the only answer. But now, Arizona looked a lot like the moon, dry and far away. And life here wasn't any better.

She squinted out the driver's side window. Dotted with the gray-greens of mesquite and cactus, the desert went on for miles. She swiped at her cheeks—her son shouldn't see her cry. Was getting stranded out here worth a few spools of thread?

Ten year-old Harold shifted in his seat. Frankie already knew how he felt about the Lakota Star quilt. As far as he was concerned, quilts were for babies. And why, he'd asked, would you need one in a place this hot?

She'd told her son the story again and again. Before her death, Grandmother had made Frankie promise to finish the coverlet depicting stories once told around tribal fires. Grandmother had been adamant—the quilt should also reflect faith in God. Today, Frankie wasn't sure about any of it, but she'd promised. If nothing else, her son should learn to keep his word.

"Rotten luck," she said, smiling at her son.

Harold's smooth face remained impassive. "We should've checked the water back at the store."

Her son had wisdom beyond his years. She patted his hand. "Good thing we wore our walking shoes, eh?" Her eyes closed, she sighed. "I'll get the cans." Harold shook his head and stared at the floorboard.

Frankie got out of the cab and went around to the truck's rusty tailgate. The blue cotton dress she wore was no match for the wind, which kicked up her skirt unless she held it down. She used her free hand for a visor and searched the road, hoping to spot the dust cloud from another vehicle. The heat of summer combined with a light wind to blast every inch of her as she scanned the horizon, but the only movement was from a couple of dust devils twirling in the distance.

She hefted the empty cans out of the bed and tapped on the truck's back window. "C'mon, it's only a mile or so to the gas station."

Getting out of the cab, her son moved like a tortoise, the way he did when he was being stubborn. With the heat bearing down on the crown of her head, she was crankier than usual. "Harold. Come on."

They started toward the gas station Frankie had hoped they could avoid. The fabric store had been bad enough. Elbow to elbow with a bunch of ladies wearing shapeless dresses and face powder the color of dust. All scooting away from her and Harold.

She'd figured the old truck had enough water in it to make it home, but she'd figured wrong. Now Stu, the sassy guy who manned the pumps at the Texaco might taunt her son—call him little Hiawatha, like last time. Stu's kid Orval, a pudgy boy with an ax to grind, had already jumped Harold once after school. Bully. Her mouth was dry. She ran her tongue across her teeth.

She glanced at Harold. He was a good boy and handsome, too, or at least he would be in a couple more years. Tall for his age, he could outrun the kids back home. And he hardly ever complained. Frankie had been thankful for it, all the way here. She smiled as she tried to match his stride. The kid probably weighed as much as the empty gallon can which knocked against his knees.

She pushed her damp bangs off her forehead. "Want me to spot you?"

"Naw. I got it." Harold's face glistened with sweat that dripped onto his brown plaid shirt.

Harold's stick-straight hair was cut short for summer. Even without braids, he looked like his father, Hank Sr. But she was determined he wouldn't turn out like his old man: prone to drink and violence. She shuddered at the memory of Hank's murder only six months before, still ashamed of the small ways she was glad. He could never hurt her or Harold again. If there was a God, her husband's passing was a gift.

Frankie kept a bright look on her face and began singing one of the Lakota songs she'd learned as a child. "C'mon, it'll pass the time," she said, and started again. In Pine Ridge, Harold was always a good sport about these things. But now he stared ahead, as if he didn't want to associate with his own mother. She walked on the road's soft shoulder and hummed to herself. Like it or not, Harold was growing up.

Ahead, the station shimmered, mirage-like—the red Texaco star a gleaming beacon. As they walked across the blacktop, heat radiated through the bottoms of her cheap sneakers. She glanced at Harold, who ran up to the concrete islands in front of the pumps. She walked faster.

The smart-mouth owner was on duty. Stu, dressed in white from head to toe, a cap sitting sideways on his pathetic crew cut. "Hey," he said to Harold. He turned to Frankie. "It'd be nice if you bought something now and then." He wiped his hands on a rag. The place reeked of oil and gas.

She pulled out her charm, the same charm she'd used to get that radiator filled a dozen times. She brushed her bangs aside. "Hey, Stu. You wouldn't mind helping a lady out would you?" Maybe she should've worn the red top with the ruffles again. Gas station attendants seemed to like red. She laughed behind her hand, an old Lakota habit she'd grown up with. When she was nervous, he couldn't stop.

But Stu's jaw muscles worked side to side. "Dry radiator, again?" He scowled at her. "I can't keep giving out free services to you people," he said. Harold stood in back of Stu, narrowing his eyes at Stu, the same way he'd seen his dad do when other men looked at her.

"All's we need is a little water to make it home," she said. Stu was such an ornery cuss—he got maybe three customers on a good day. The wind came up and gusted against her cheeks, then died. Frankie tasted dirt.

They all turned back toward the road. A rumble and dirt-colored cloud trailed a government truck. Stu waved them back. "I got a real customer. You'll have to wait."

Frankie and Harold moved a couple feet and set down the cans. She poked Harold and pointed to a drinking fountain. "Go get a drink," she said.

The white pickup, with "Bureau of Land Management" in raised letters on the door, braked to a stop. She folded her arms. Let Stu attend to Mr. Important.

A light-skinned but dark-haired lanky man stepped out. His eyes were hard to see under his hat's brim. He wore cowboy boots and an agate belt buckle. The buckle gave him away. Most of her male relatives wore the same type of agate buckle. He had to be part Lakota—and who knew what else. The man, in his tan government uniform and all, sparked something in Frankie. His voice was deep, melodic. "Can you fill it up?" The man wasn't sarcastic the way Hank Sr. always was. No, this guy was more than polite and didn't let Stu's attitude chase him up a tree. The man nodded at the most expensive gas pump. "I reckon the government can spring for ethyl," the man said.

Stu nodded, although he seemed a tad disappointed he was serving another Indian. Stu went to work, the gas pump dinging. "Can't say I've seen you round here." Stu pulled a squeegee across the bug-encrusted windshield. "You new?"

The stranger smiled; his teeth were white and straight. "Nick Parker," he said, touching his hat's brim. "Just transferred down from Nebraska." He took off the hat and used his forearm to mop his brow. "I'm still getting used to the heat."

Harold snorted. Frankie elbowed her son, but it was too late. The man turned. "You from the Rez?"

Frankie and Harold looked at each other. The local Pima-Maricopa reservation?

Harold shook his head. "Nope." He raised his chin. "Lakota."

Frankie's throat burned, but she couldn't force herself to move away from the stranger. "Go on, son, and get a drink." She pointed again to the fountain.

"Ma! Stop treating me like a kid." He sat on the curb.

Nick seemed interested in the boy. "Where you from then?" He sat next to Harold, arms resting across his knees.

A guy who likes kids, Frankie thought. She watched out of the corner of her eye as the man spoke with her son. Nick's thick, coppery hair swept back from his forehead. But the handsome ones could be dangerous.

Stu pulled the gas nozzle out and hung it on the pump. He came over. "Want me to check the water and oil?" He shot Frankie and Harold a look. "You can overheat pretty easy on a day like this."

Nick laughed, and his eyes brightened and sent a chill up Frankie's back. "Sure," he said. "Don't want to overheat out here, right?"

Right. Her breath caught, as if she were viewing the Milky Way for the first time. Whoa. She didn't believe in love at first sight anymore, especially when love later grew fists.

An awkward moment passed, as if he'd heard her thoughts. He stood up and turned to the pair. "Are you here to stay or just passing through?"

Frankie drew her shoulders back. The man stood straight, proud; his eyes were a whiskey shade of brown. It would be easy to get sucked in, too easy. She locked her heart. But in the next moment, Frankie let the wind take her caution. "We're hoping to make our home here." She laughed, forcing her hand to stay at her side. "It's the wrong time of year to be snowbirds." She wished again she'd worn red. "As Harold said, Lakota," she said. "We're Lakota."

Nick's eyes lit up. "Not many Lakota this far from South Dakota. What made you want to come live in the desert?"

Frankie shrugged. Why they'd left South Dakota was complicated—too complicated to talk about. "We thought we'd like the nice, cool Arizona summers," she said. "I'm Frankie and this is my son, Harold."

Stu barged into the conversation again. "That'll be three dollars," he said. Nick dug out a bill and handed it to Stu.

"I'll get your change," Stu said.

Nick turned to Frankie. "Huh." He paused. "What a coincidence. Growing up, I spent my summers at Pine Ridge." He used his hat like a fan. "It's got to be a hundred and ten."

Stu corrected him. "Hunert and eleven."

Nick grinned. "Hot enough to fry an egg on the sidewalk."

Slouched beside a gas pump, Harold broke his silence. "Ma overheated the truck 'bout a mile back," he said, pointing to the water cans. "She just had to buy thread. Today." Frankie gave him a look, but this was a good sign. If Harold said more than two words, it meant he liked you.

Nick picked up the cans. "Let's get these filled," he said. He looked deep into Frankie's eyes and held his gaze steady. "Could I give you a lift back to your truck?"

———

Nick spooled out the water hose and filled up the cans, studying the young woman and her son. Prettiest girl he'd ever laid eyes on. Her free-falling black hair danced in the wind as she said, "Oh, no, we can make it all right. But thank you." She looked away, giving Nick a moment to appreciate her profile. Water overflowed onto his boot. It's what he got for gawking. He prayed for forgiveness.

She spoke softly. "Harold, get a drink before we go, OK honey?"

Harold dragged himself to the drinking fountain attached to the side of a soda pop cooler outside the repair bay. For five cents, the cooler's top slid open and you could pull out an ice cold drink. Summers in Pine Ridge, Nick and his buddies had pilfered a soda or two from a machine like that. Then, got beat up by a bully named Moose.

He let the water hose reel itself back in and picked up the full cans. He faced the woman named Frankie, the wind pressing her thin blue dress against her body. "These things weigh a ton," he said. Her figure was better than the Rodeo Princess up at Prescott. He said, "You got a bum radiator?"

Frankie shrugged. "Got to get that thing fixed."

Nick hoped he wasn't too pushy, but he didn't try to stop himself from being drawn in, either. "Your old man won't help you?" He set down the water, which sloshed onto his boots again.

She ran her fingers through her hair. "Not exactly." Her hands were plain, capable and strong, not fancied up with polished nails or jewelry or even a wedding ring. Nick liked simplicity. A practical sort, not like his ex, Carolyn. She'd about driven them into the poorhouse with her beauty parlor treatments and whatnot. He preferred her story to Carolyn's version, hers blamed Nick and a friend named alcohol.

The bottle had claimed his dad and half his relatives at Pine Ridge. Nick had nearly ten years sober, and had broken the Parker family tradition—Carolyn hadn't give him enough credit.

He tried to make eye contact, but Frankie stared at the horizon. "You planning on staying out here?"

Her gaze flitted to Harold at the drinking fountain and back again. "The kid's dad died in South Dakota." She paused, as if thinking up a good explanation. "Hank Sr., that's my husband, used to say he had relatives here, so I thought, 'Why not?'" She took a breath, and finally returned his stare.

He took off his hat and got lost in her deep brown eyes. He said, "Sorry. Got to be tough on the boy." He wanted to ask if she was seeing anyone, tell her he liked her simple beauty, offer to cook her dinner sometime. His tongue balked.

Before he could say anything, Stu's voice rang out. "You thievin' injun, pay up!"

⚬⚬⚬

Harold raced past Frankie and Nick, with Stu in pursuit. A wet stain down Harold's shirt looked suspicious. Frankie fingered the spools of thread in her pocket, wondering if Stu was in a bartering mood as Harold hid behind his mother.

The attendant wagged a finger. "All right, Frankie Chasing Bear," he said. "That'll be a nickel. And I've got a mind to charge you for the water. That boy of yours is getting to be a real headache."

Nick gave Frankie a puzzled look, but dug into his pocket. "Here," he said, producing a nickel. "Indian head, no less."

Stu took the money.

Frankie pulled Harold around to face her. She spoke in a low, even tone. "You did this?"

Harold looked ready to cry. "No, Ma." He raised his tee shirt to reveal his waistband. "See?"

Frankie nodded. "Look Stu, my kid didn't take anything."

Stu narrowed his eyes. "How do I know he didn't stash it somewhere?"

Nick stepped toward Stu. "The kid says he didn't steal it." He dug out more change. "But we'd like cold ones for the road." Nick strode to the cooler and brought back three bottles.

Stu glared, but nodded and straightened his cap.

Nick handed a cold, sweaty bottle to Frankie. "Thank you." She wouldn't let on, but RC Cola tasted like heaven. She elbowed Harold. "Where are your manners?"

"Thanks." Harold tipped back his soda and began walking back down the road.

"Harold! Wait!"

But Harold waved her off and kept walking. The kid could be as stubborn as his dad.

Nick brought her attention back. "Let me take you back to your rig."

Frankie hoped her son's moodiness wouldn't embarrass the both of them. "Harold's got a mind of his own," she said. "Some days I think one of us won't live to see Christmas." She smoothed her bangs with her palm. "Sure, I'll take a lift."

Nick smiled too. His forehead and cheekbones had a noble hint that tugged at Frankie. She wanted to ask him which Lakota band his mother was from, was he related to any of the famous chiefs. He tilted his head toward the truck. "C'mon, let's get that rascal." He held the driver's side door open.

Frankie climbed into the cab and slid across the bench seat, still gripping the soda bottle. Nick got in after her and started the truck. When he slammed the door, she picked up a whiff of sage.

Abingdon fiction™

A Novel Approach To Faith

Enjoy these entertaining reads from Abingdon Fiction

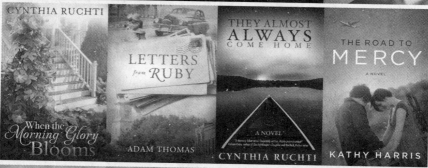

Find
Abing

Follow us on Twitter
@AbingdonFiction